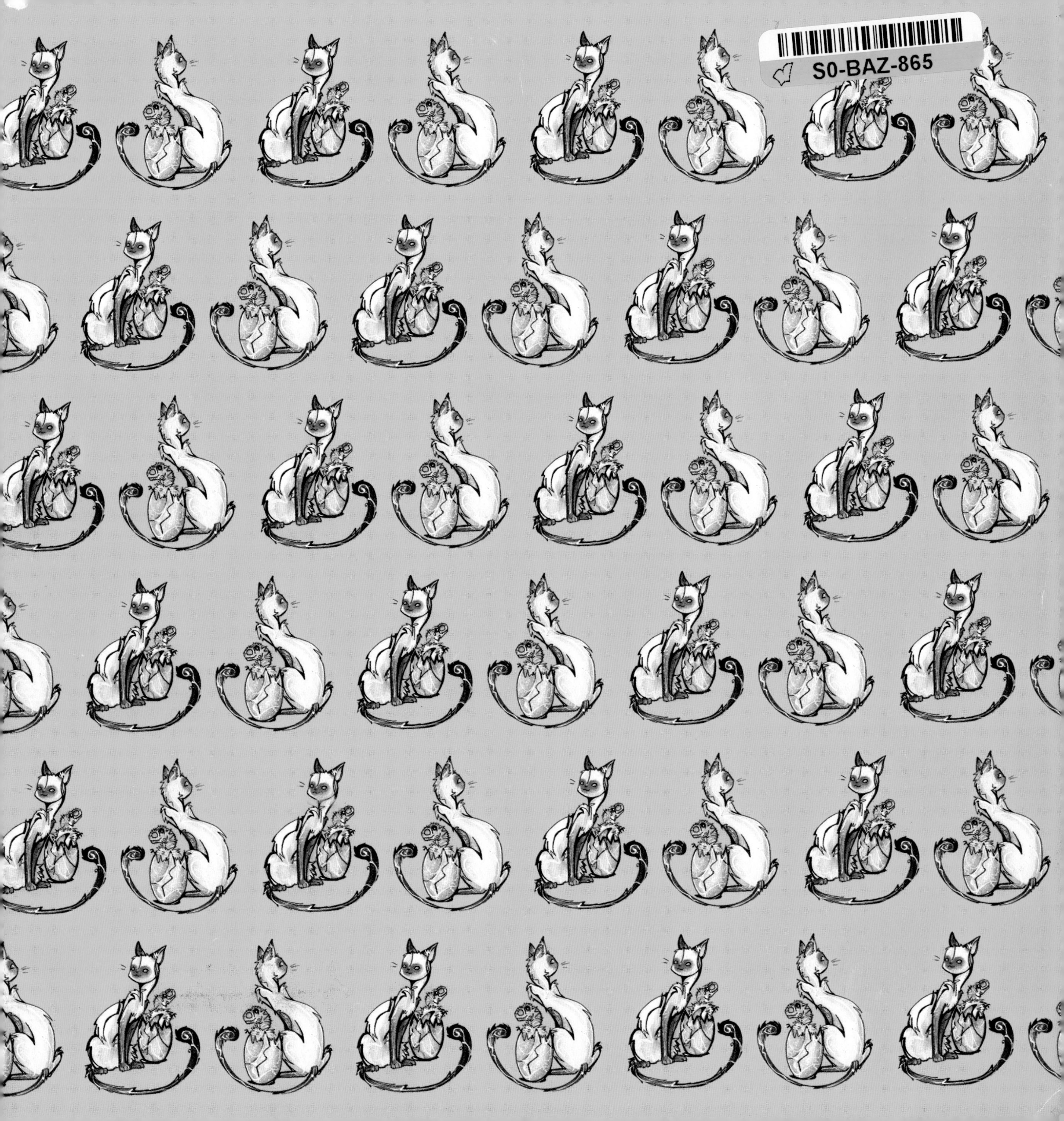

Kitty & Dino

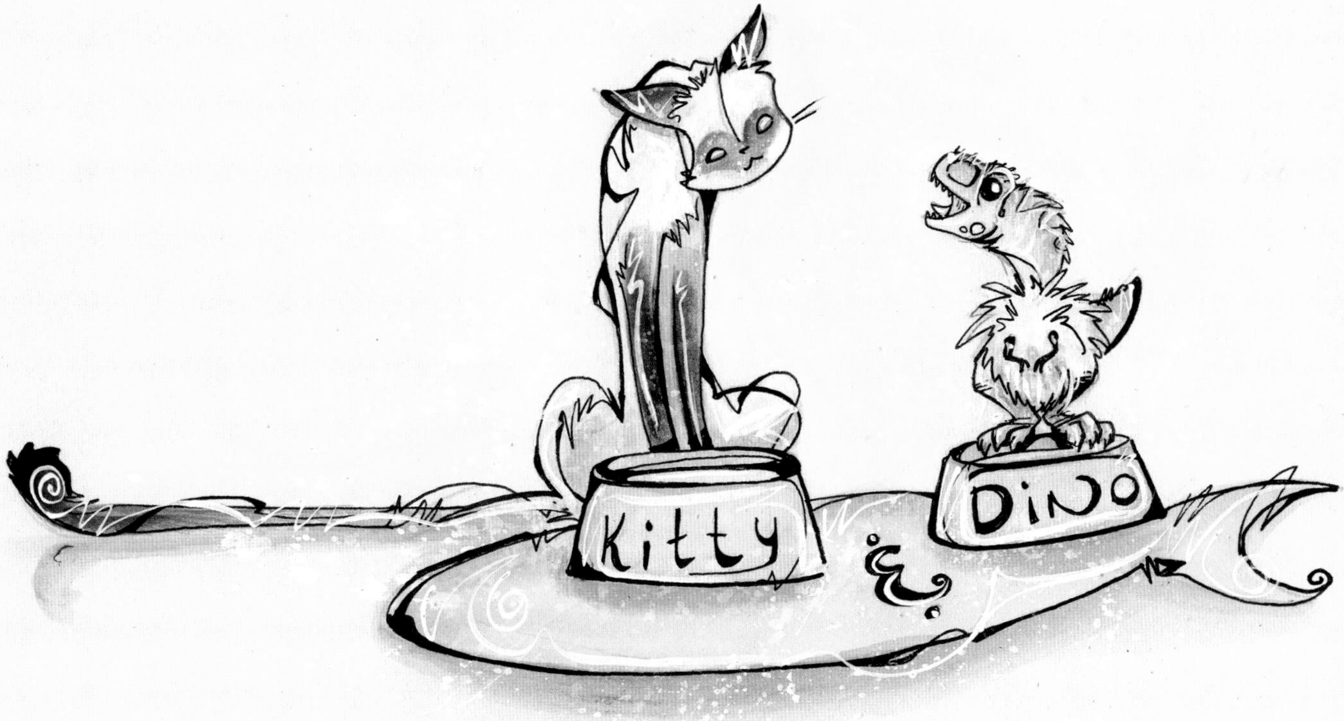
Kitty
Dino

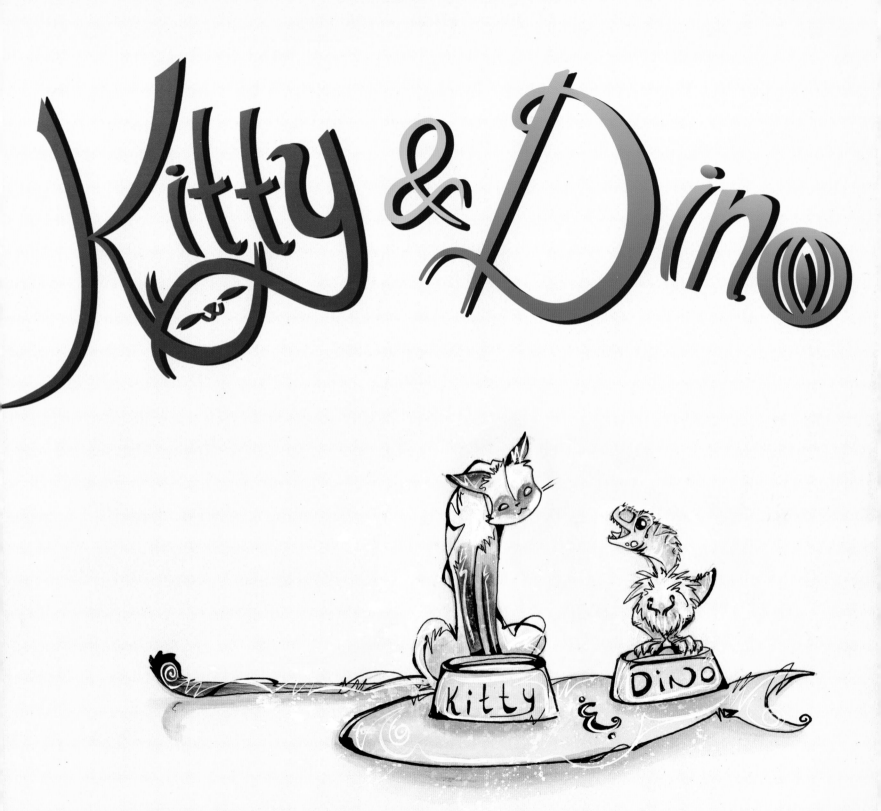

Illustrated by Sara Richard

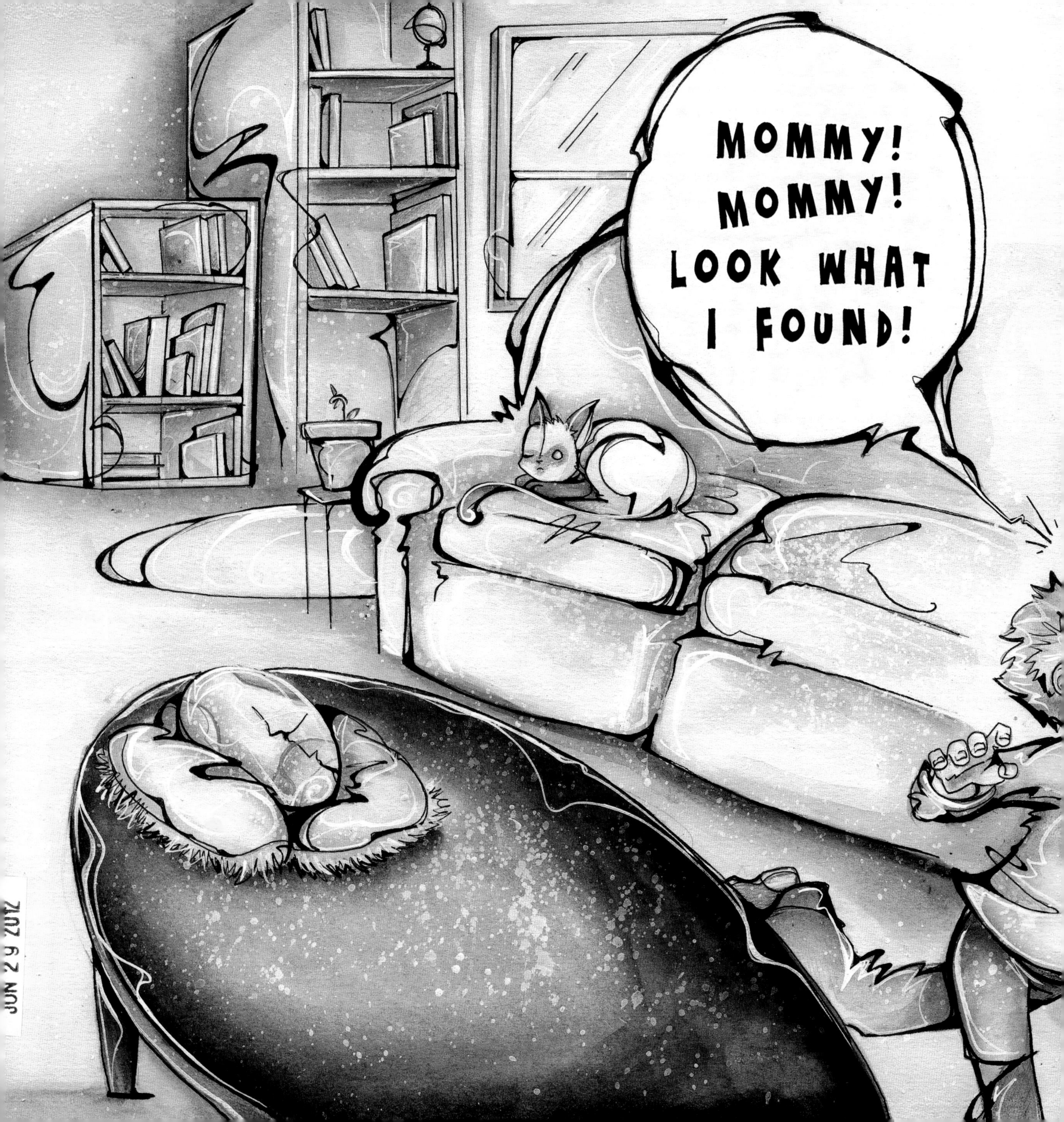
MOMMY! MOMMY! LOOK WHAT I FOUND!

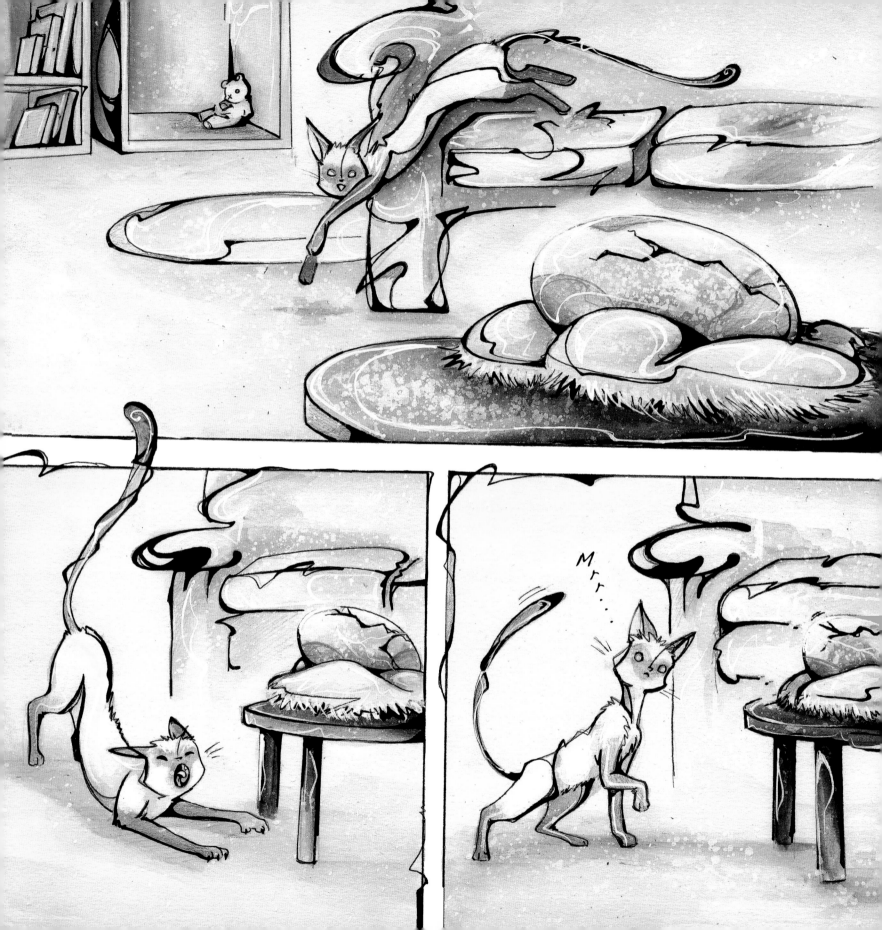

Mrr . . .

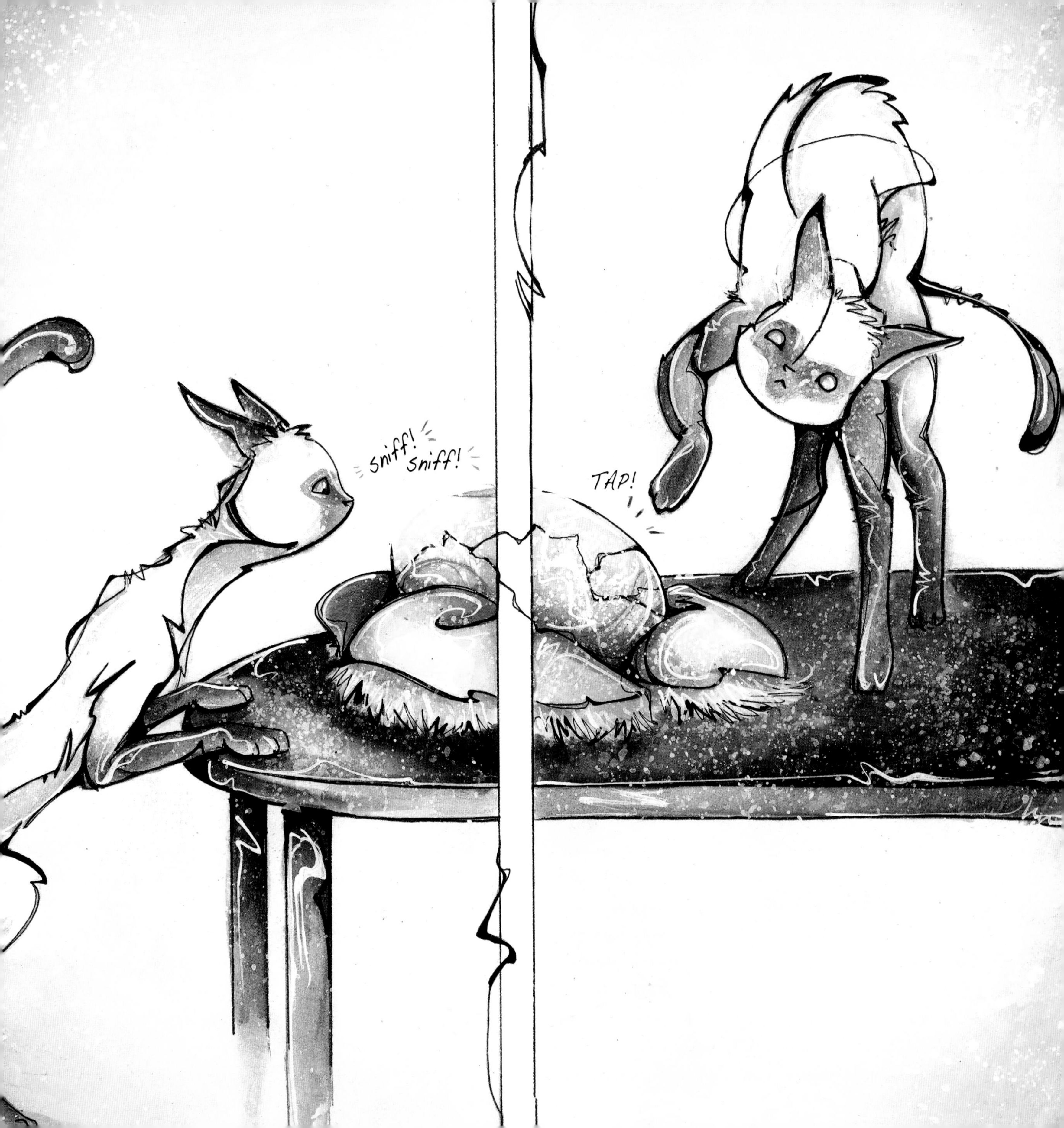
sniff!
sniff!
TAP!

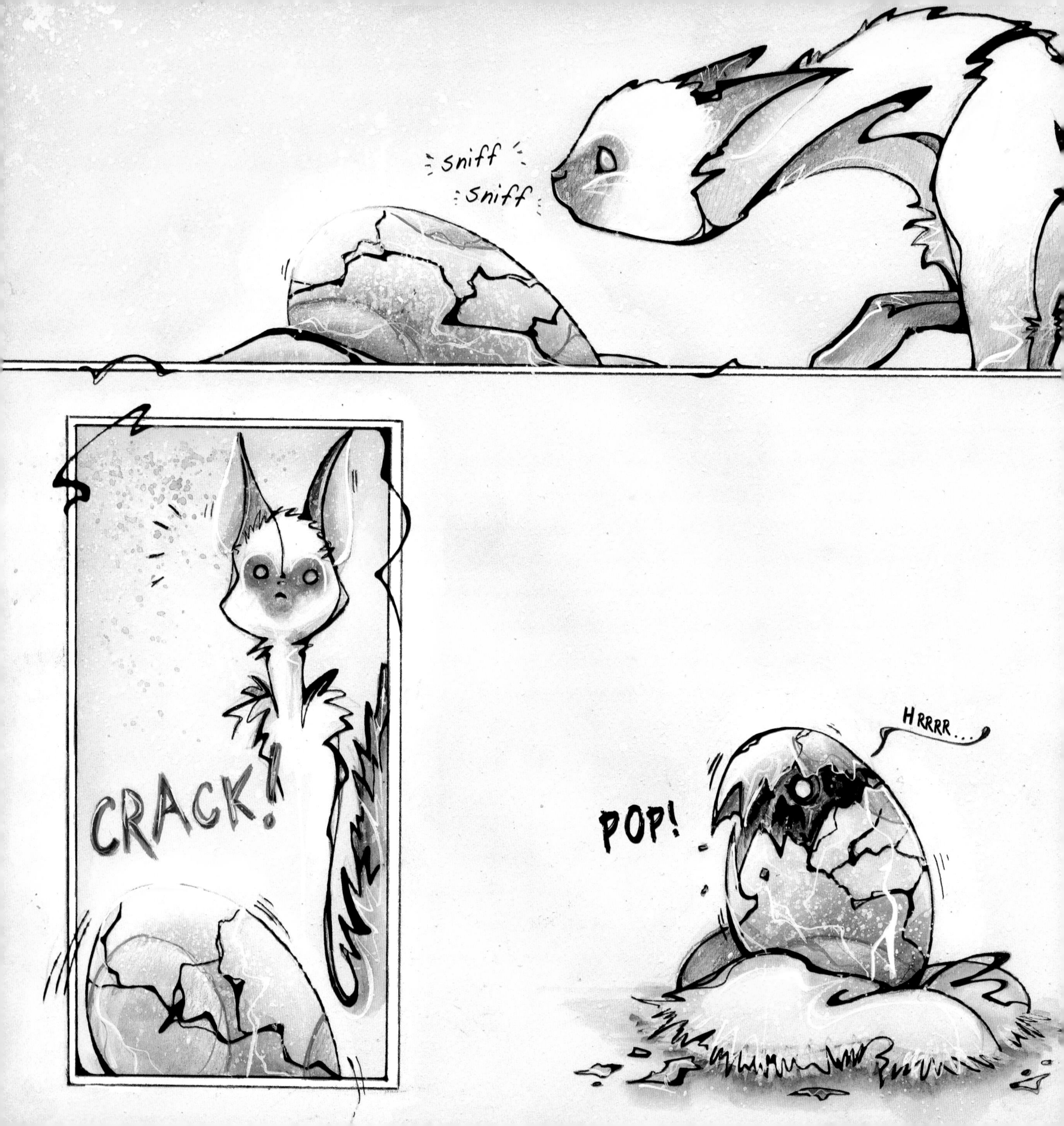
sniff
sniff
CRACK!
POP!
HRRRR...

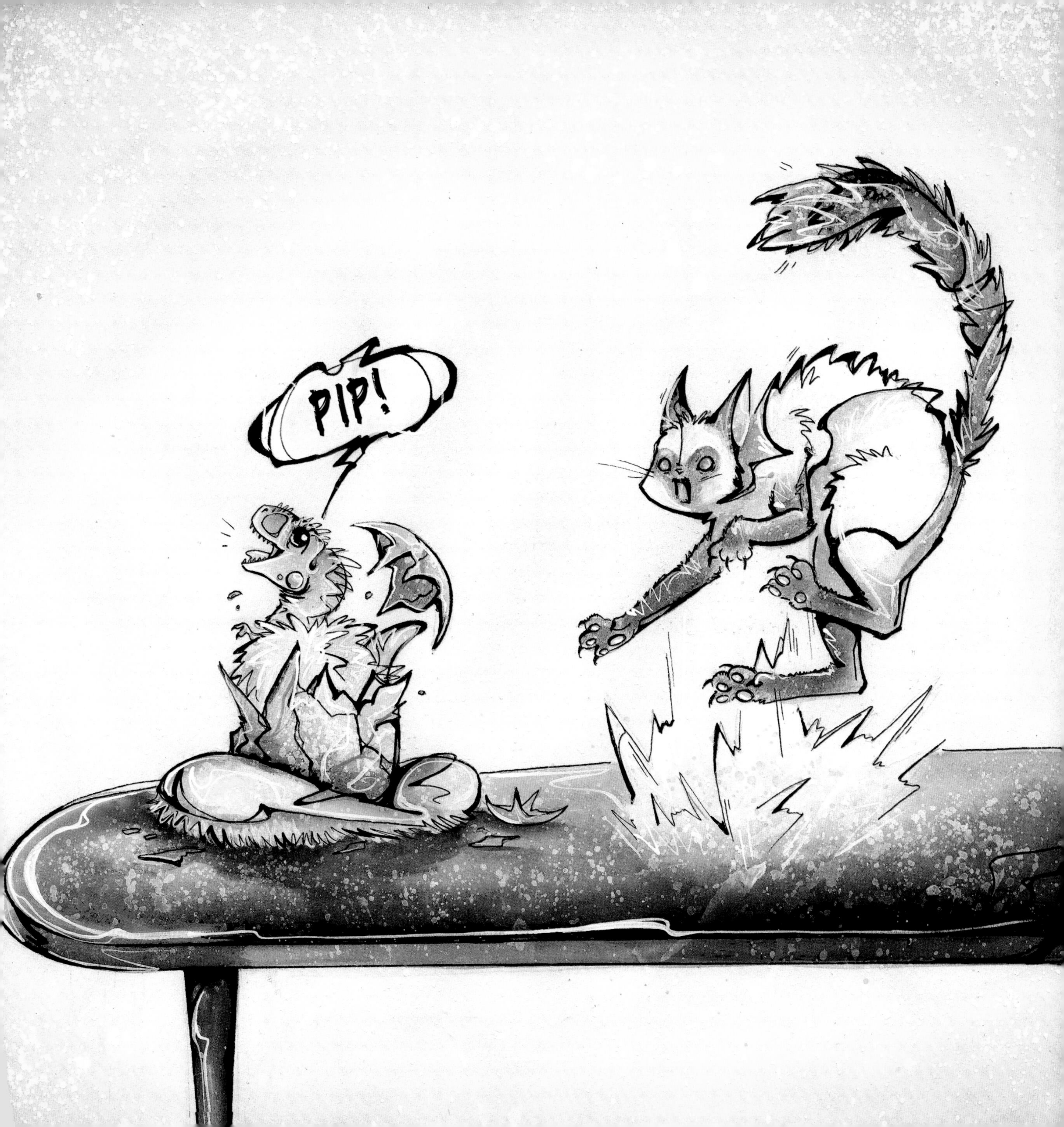
PIP!

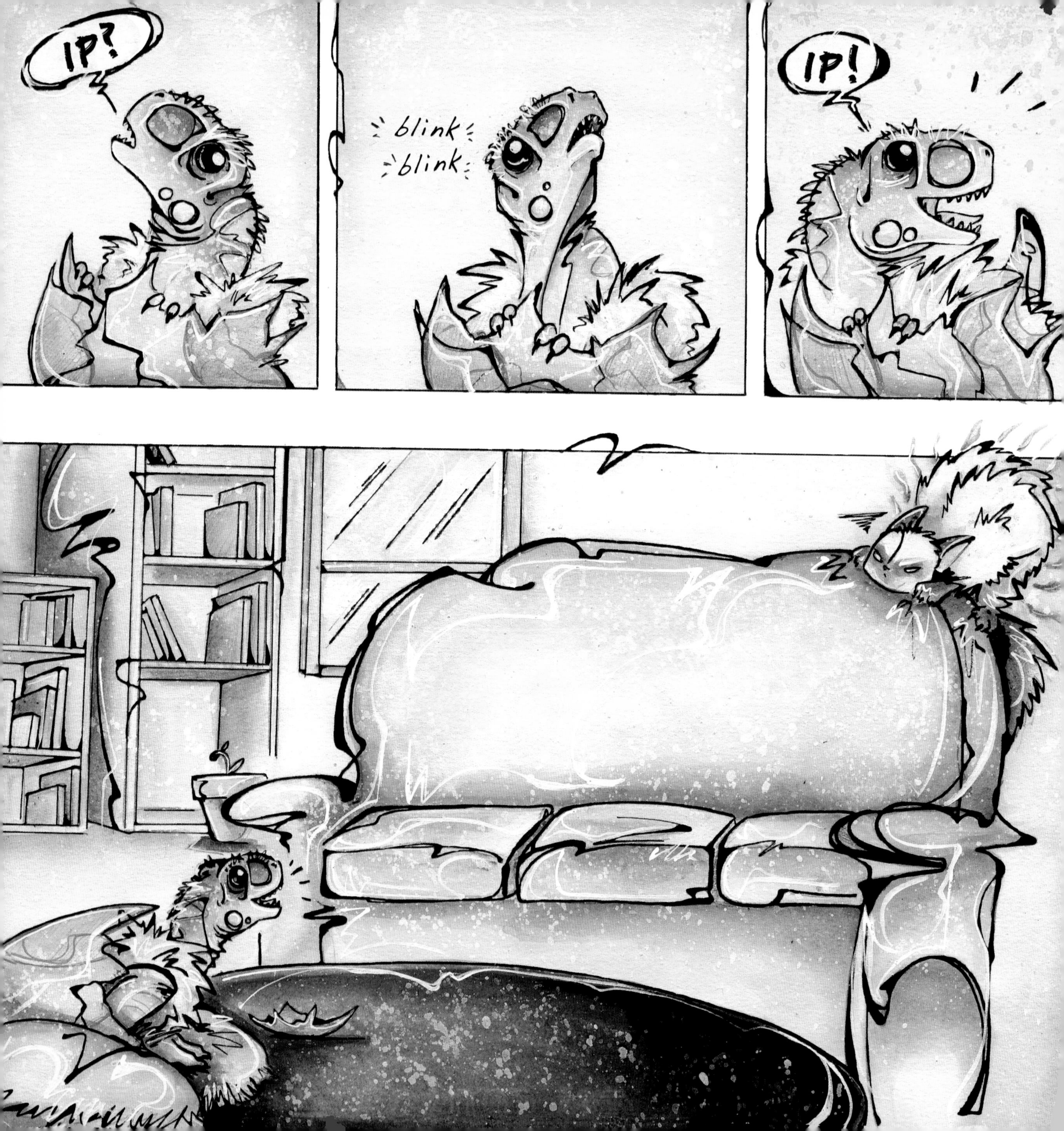

IP?
blink
blink
IP!

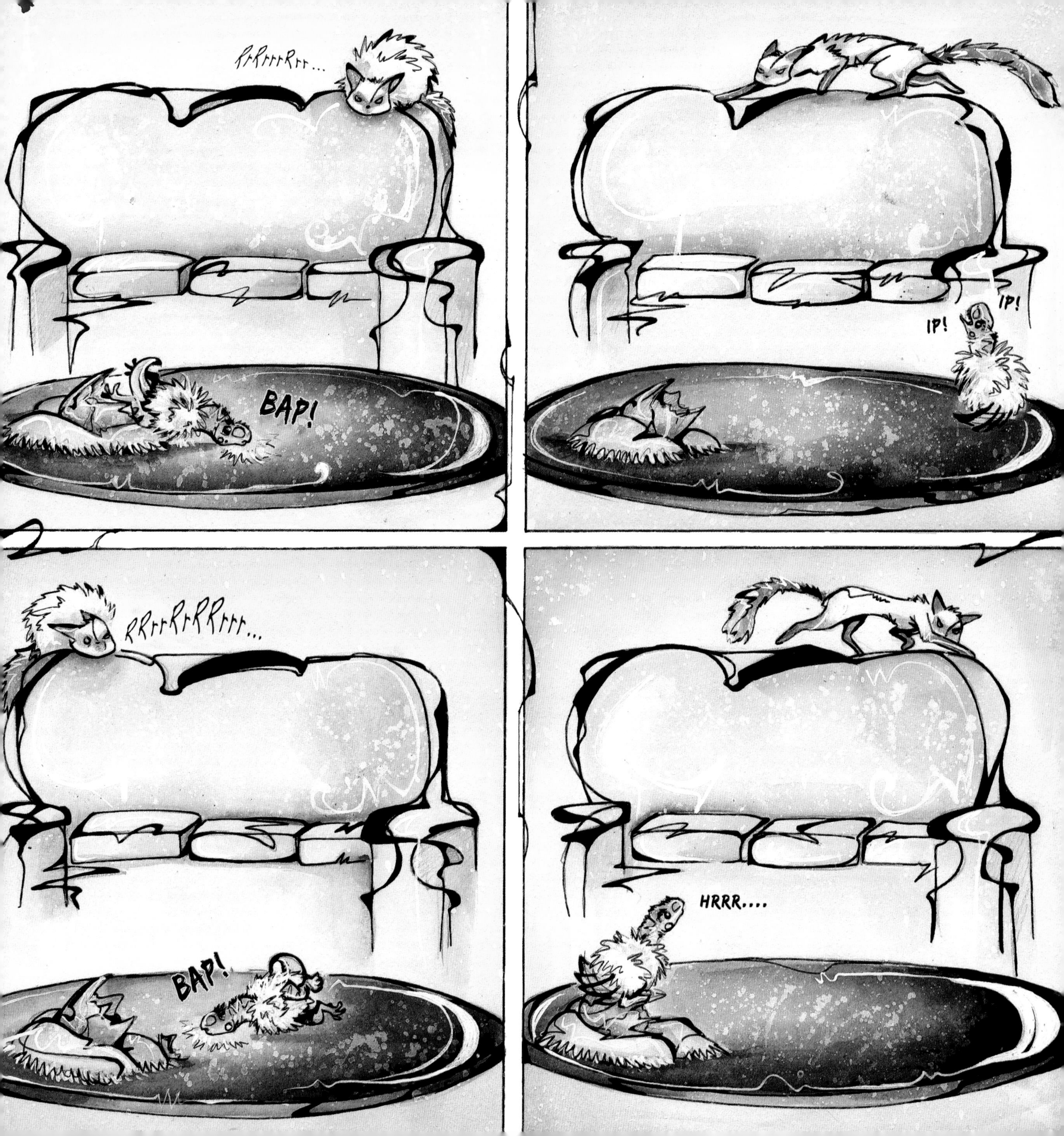

RrRrrrRrr...
BAP!
IP!
IP!
RRrrRrRRrrr...
BAP!
HRRR....

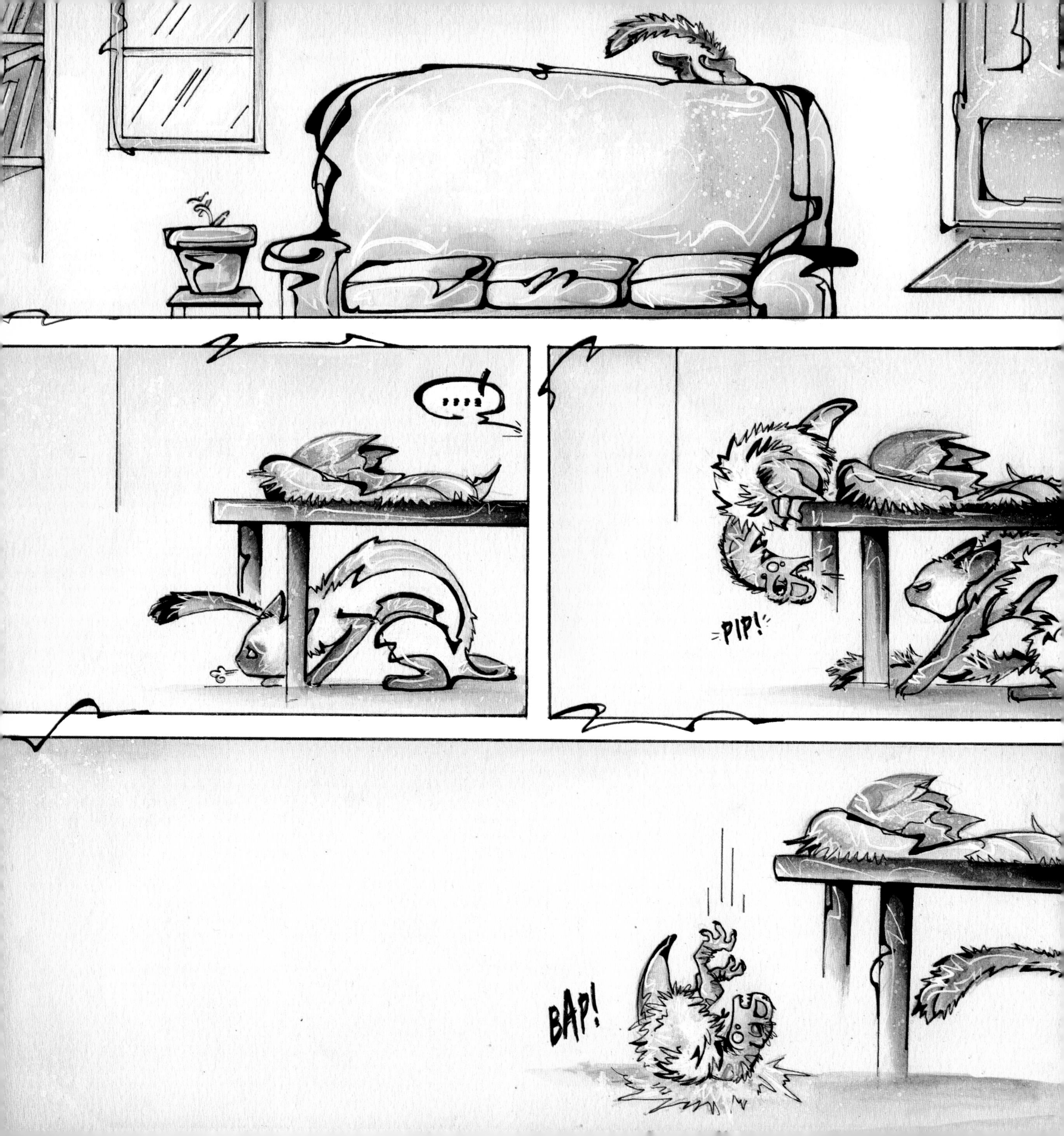
....
PIP!
BAP!

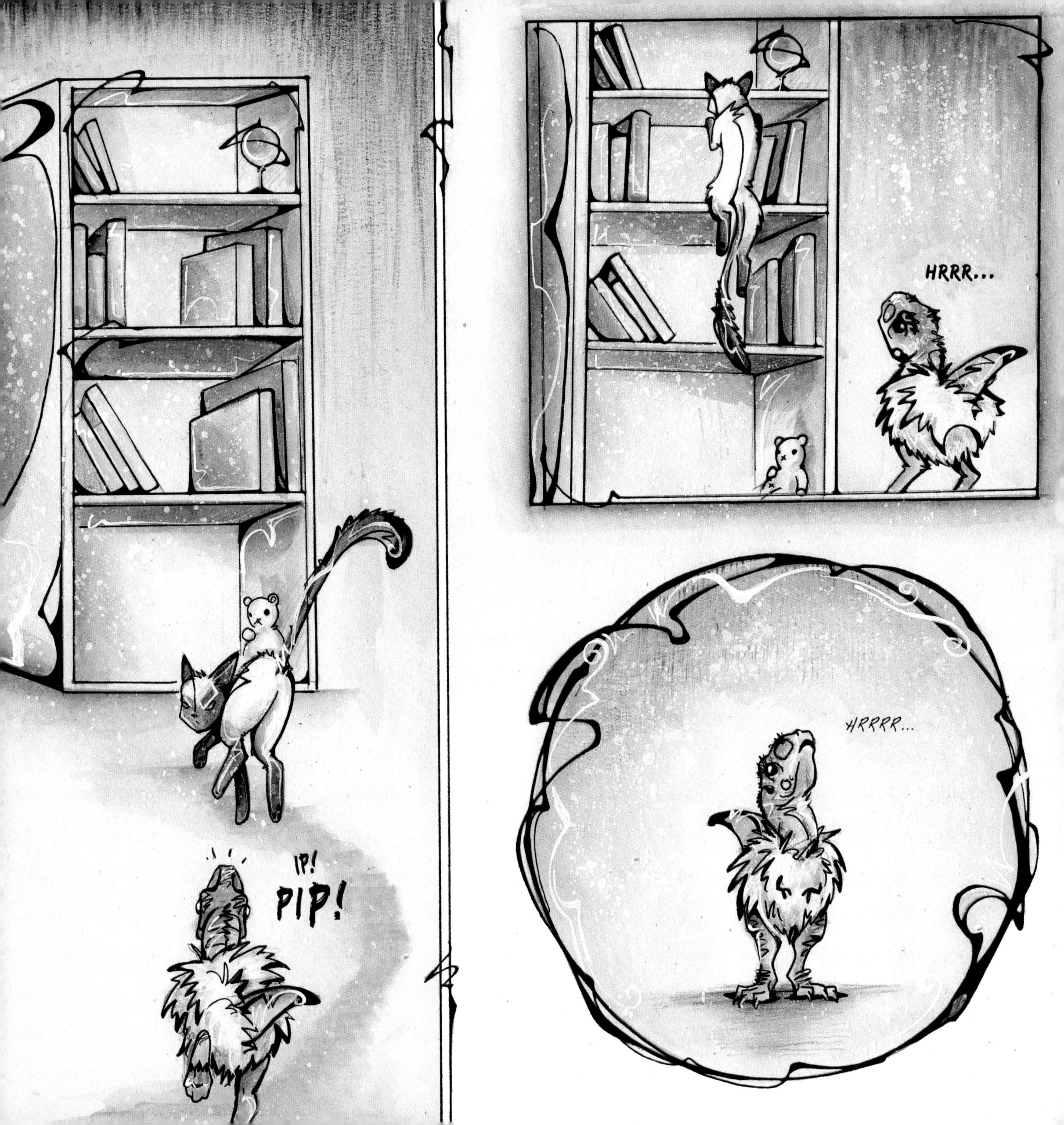
IP!
PIP!
HRRR...
HRRRR...

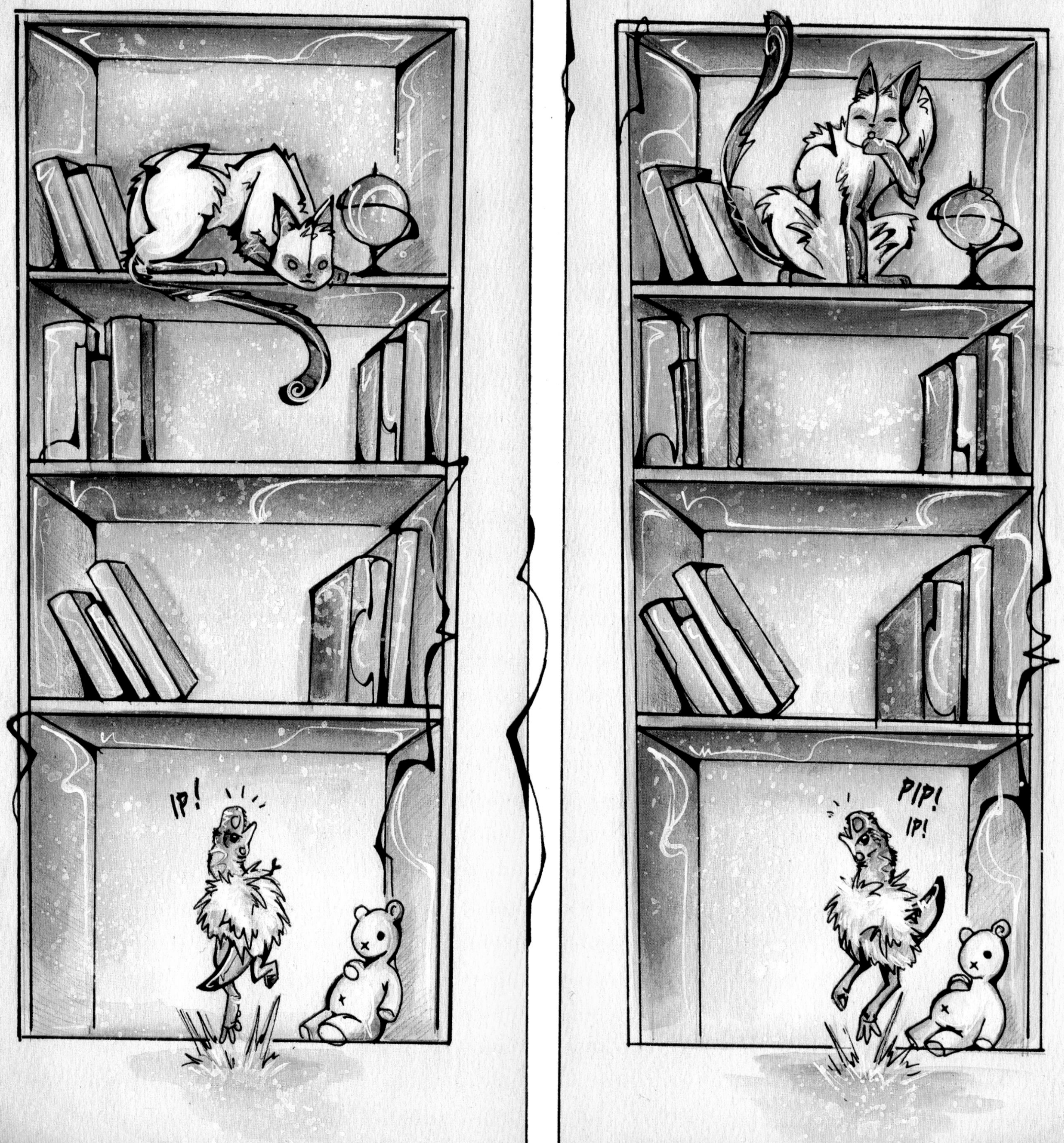
IP!
PIP!
IP!

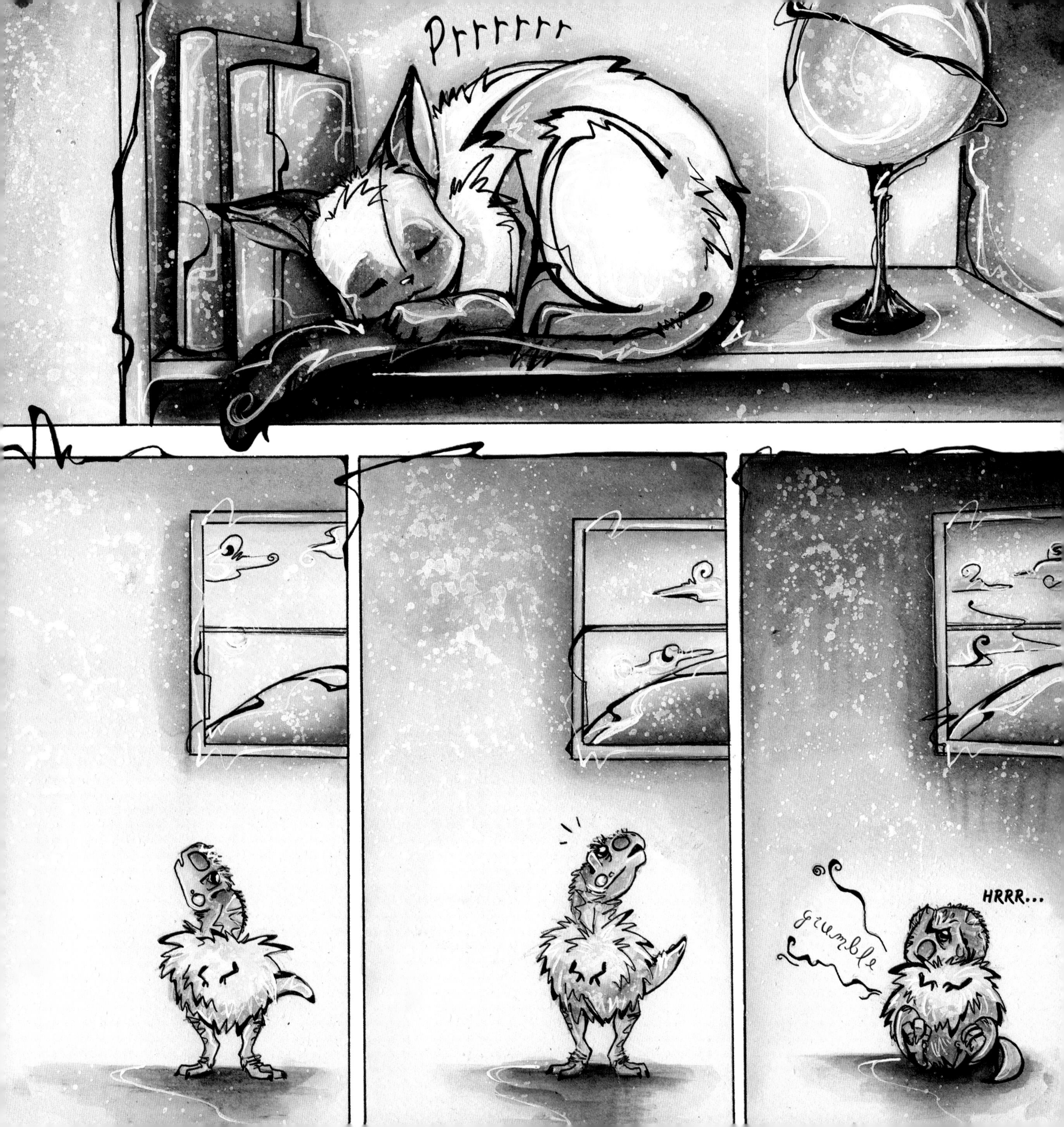
Prrrrrr
grumble
HRRR...

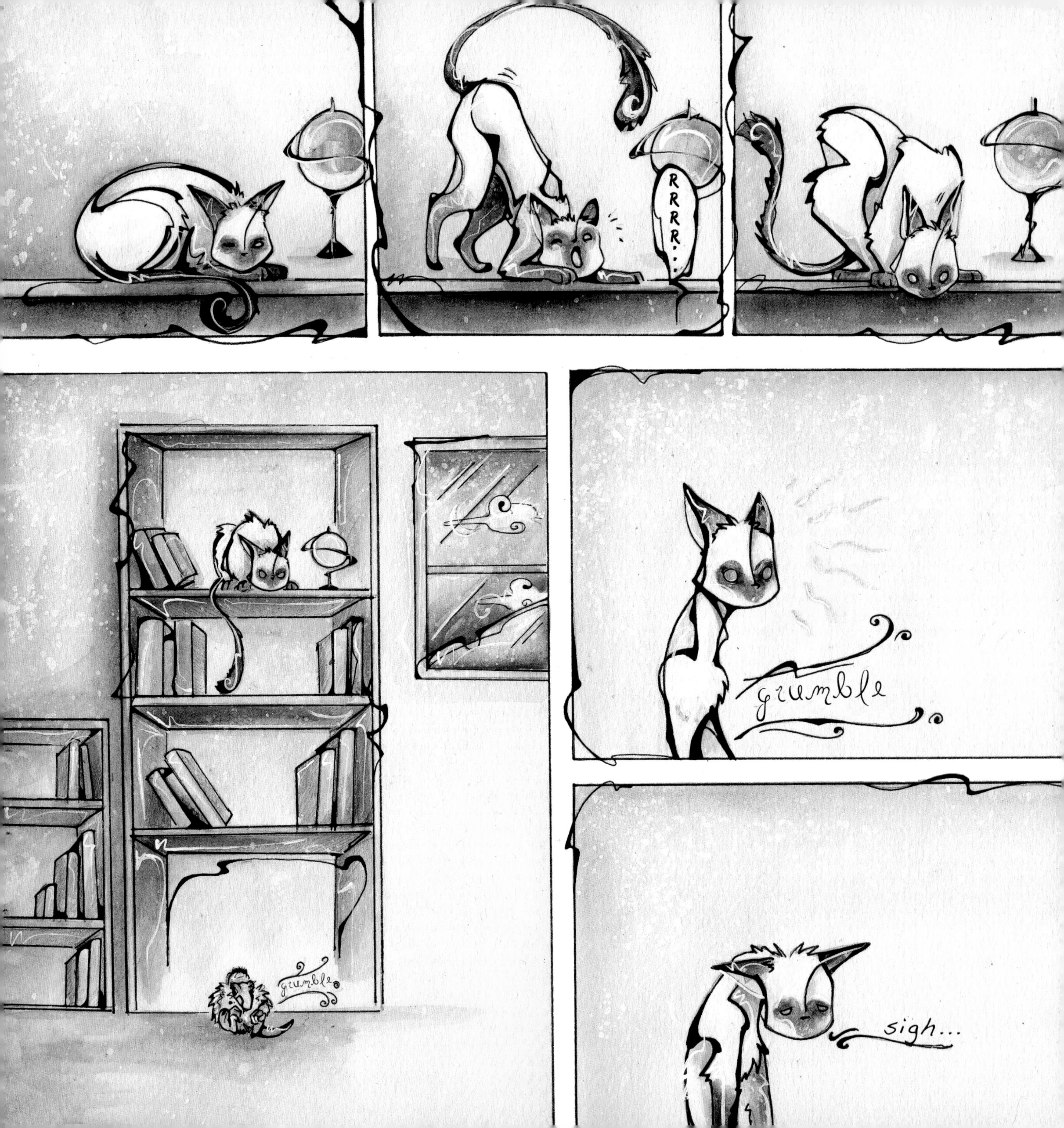
RRRR..
grumble
grumble
sigh...

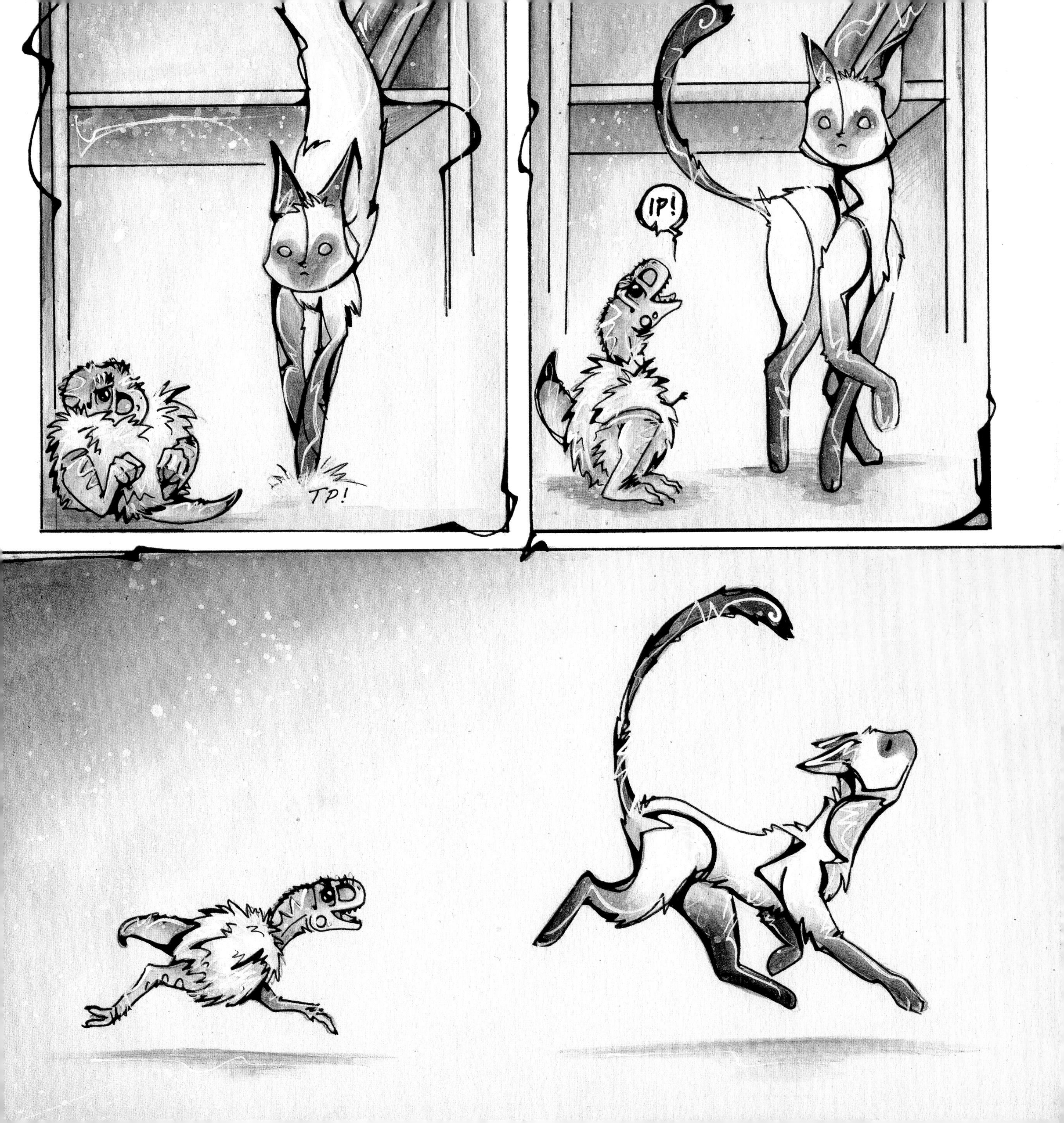
TP!
!P!

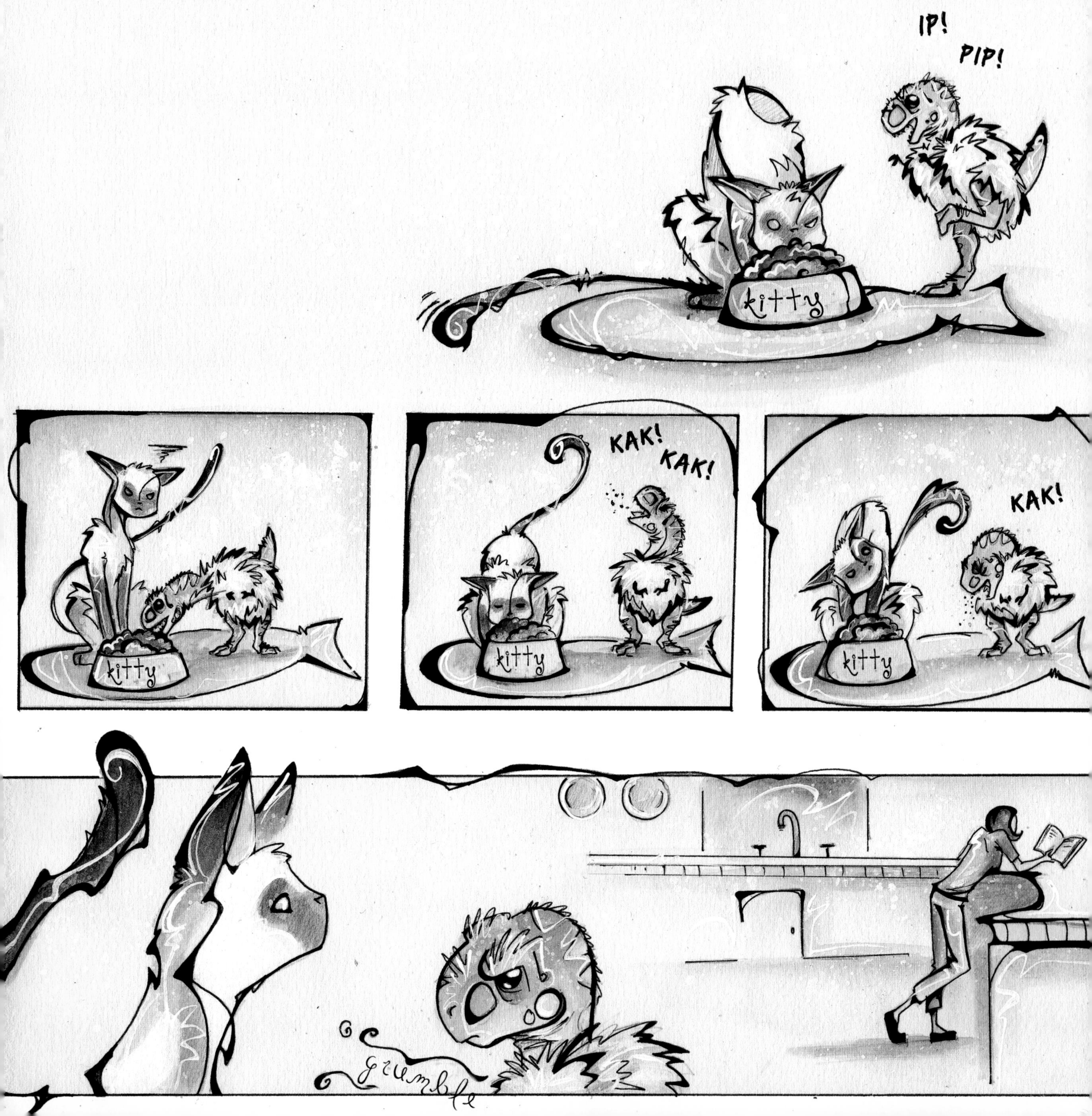
IP!
PIP!
kitty
kitty
KAK!
KAK!
kitty
KAK!
kitty
grumble

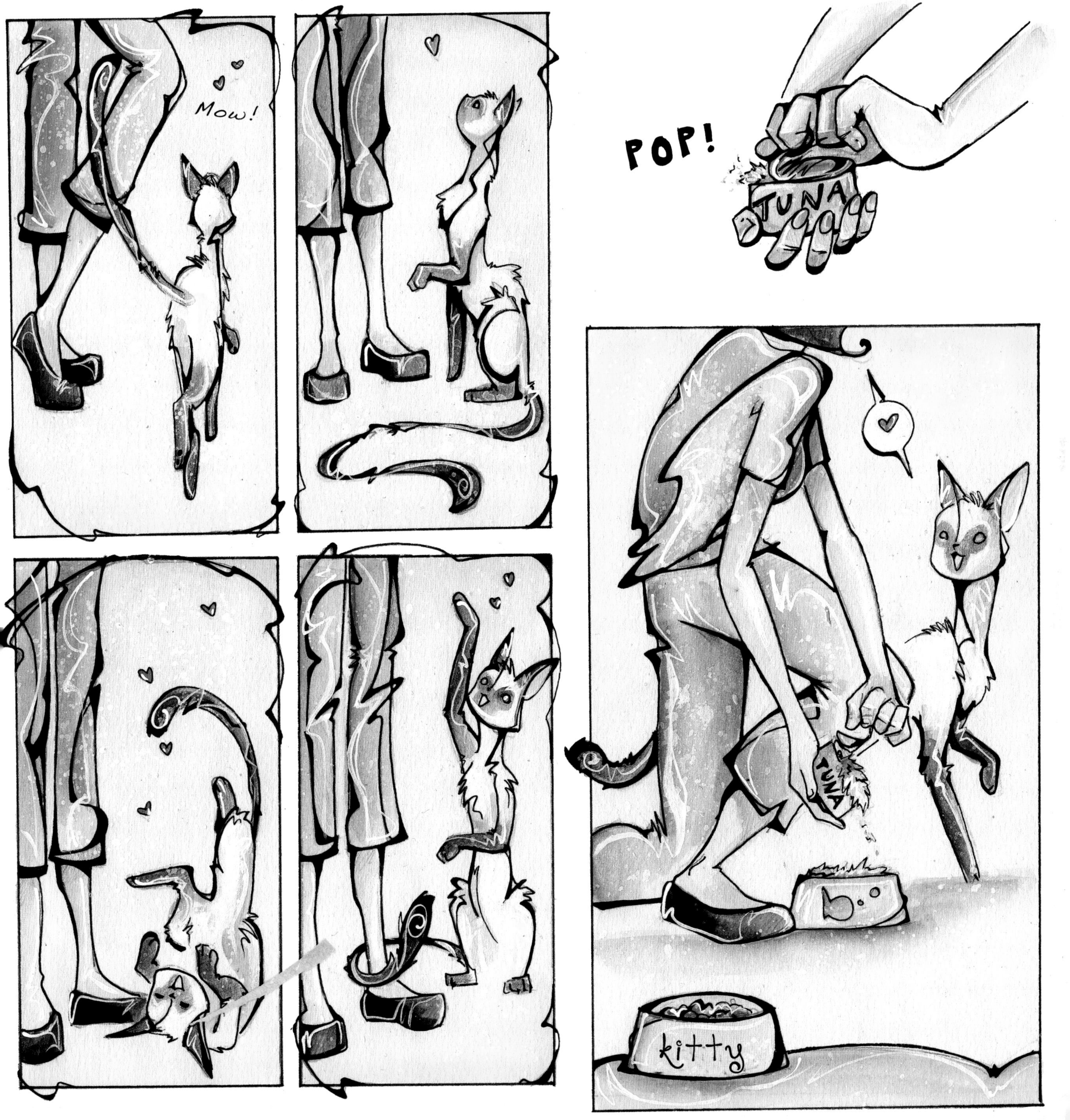
Mow!
POP!
TUNA
TUNA
kitty

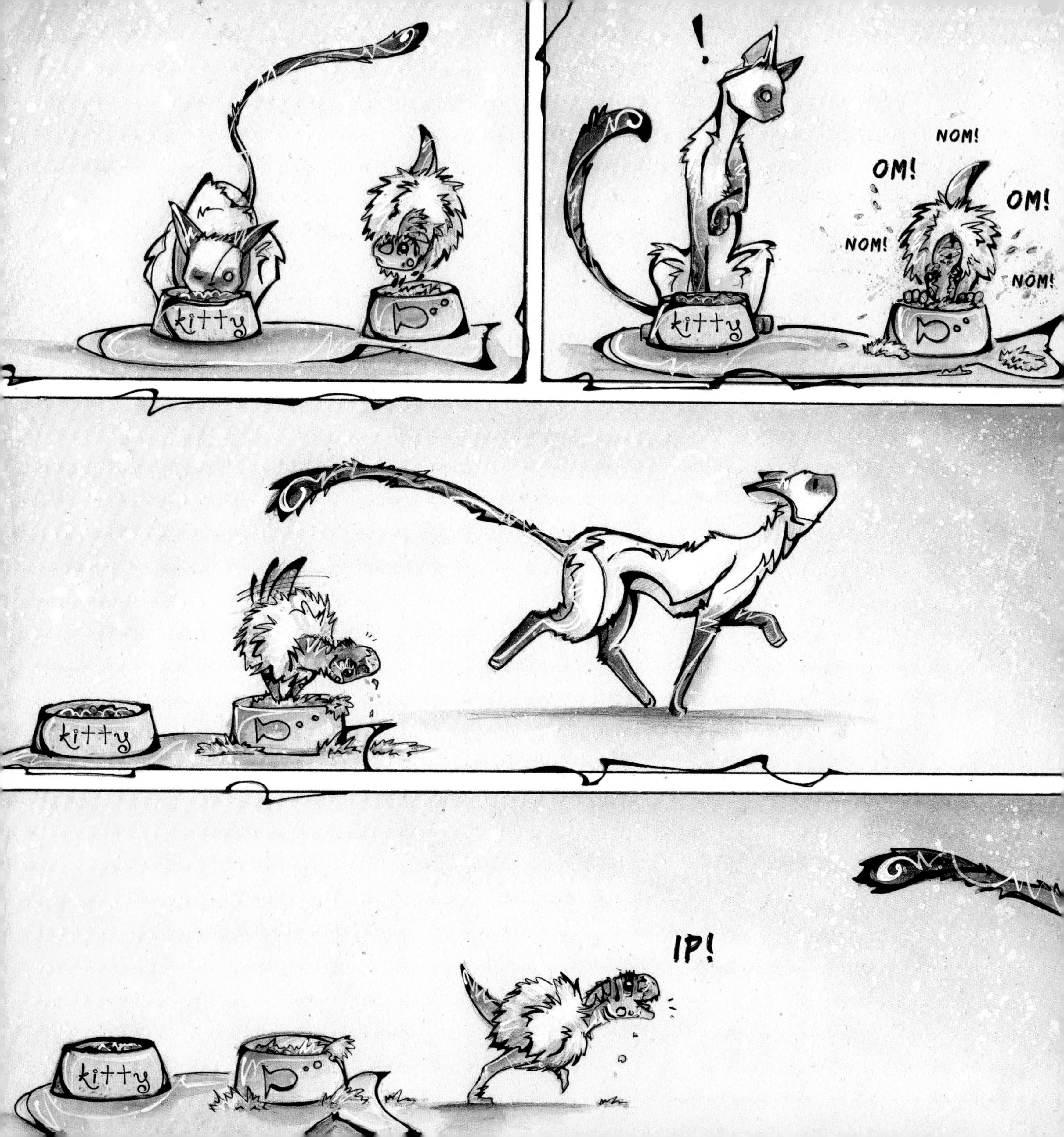
kitty
kitty
!
NOM!
OM!
OM!
NOM!
NOM!
kitty
kitty
IP!

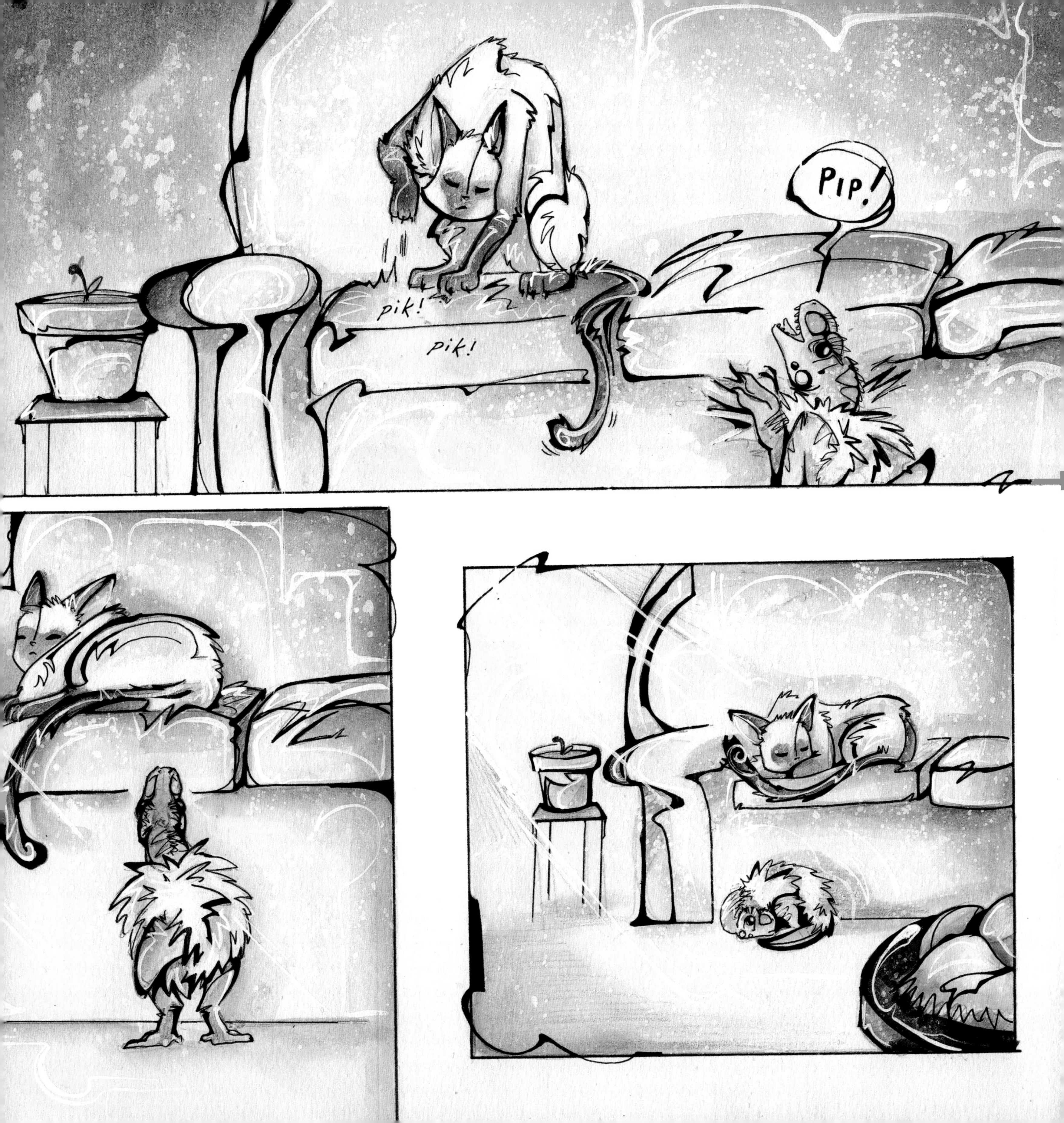
pik!
pik!
PIP!

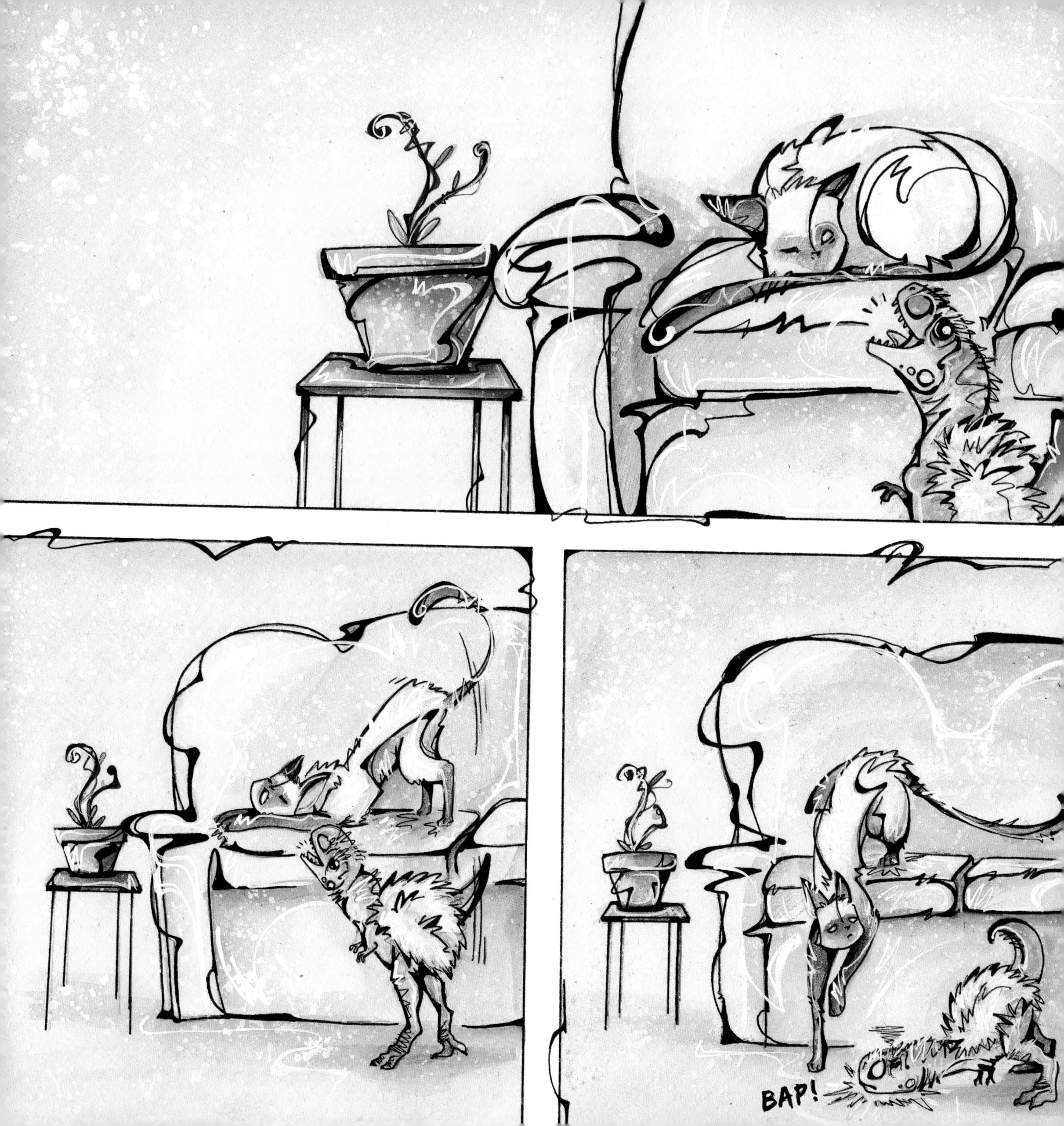

BAP!

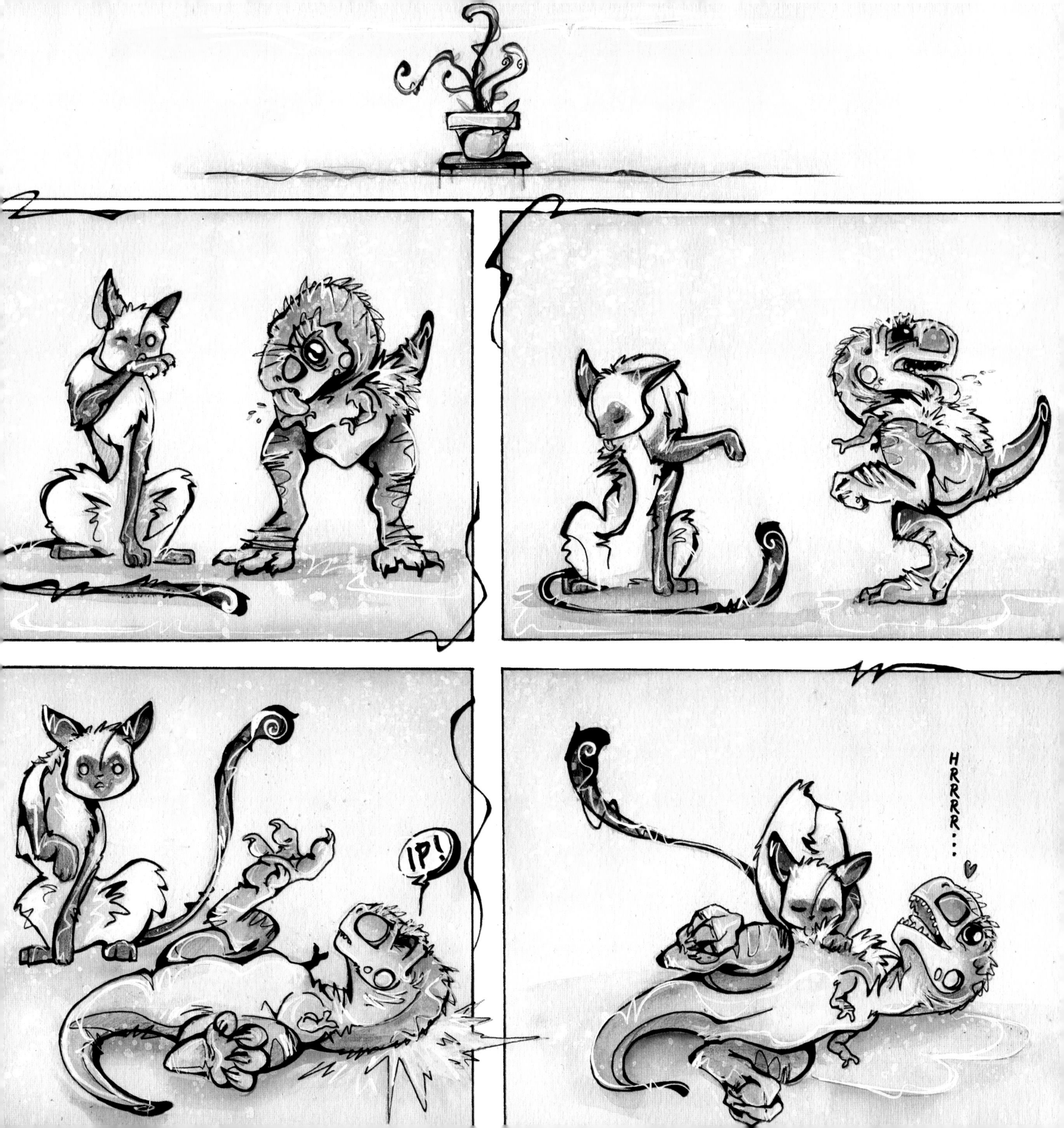
IP!
HRRRR...

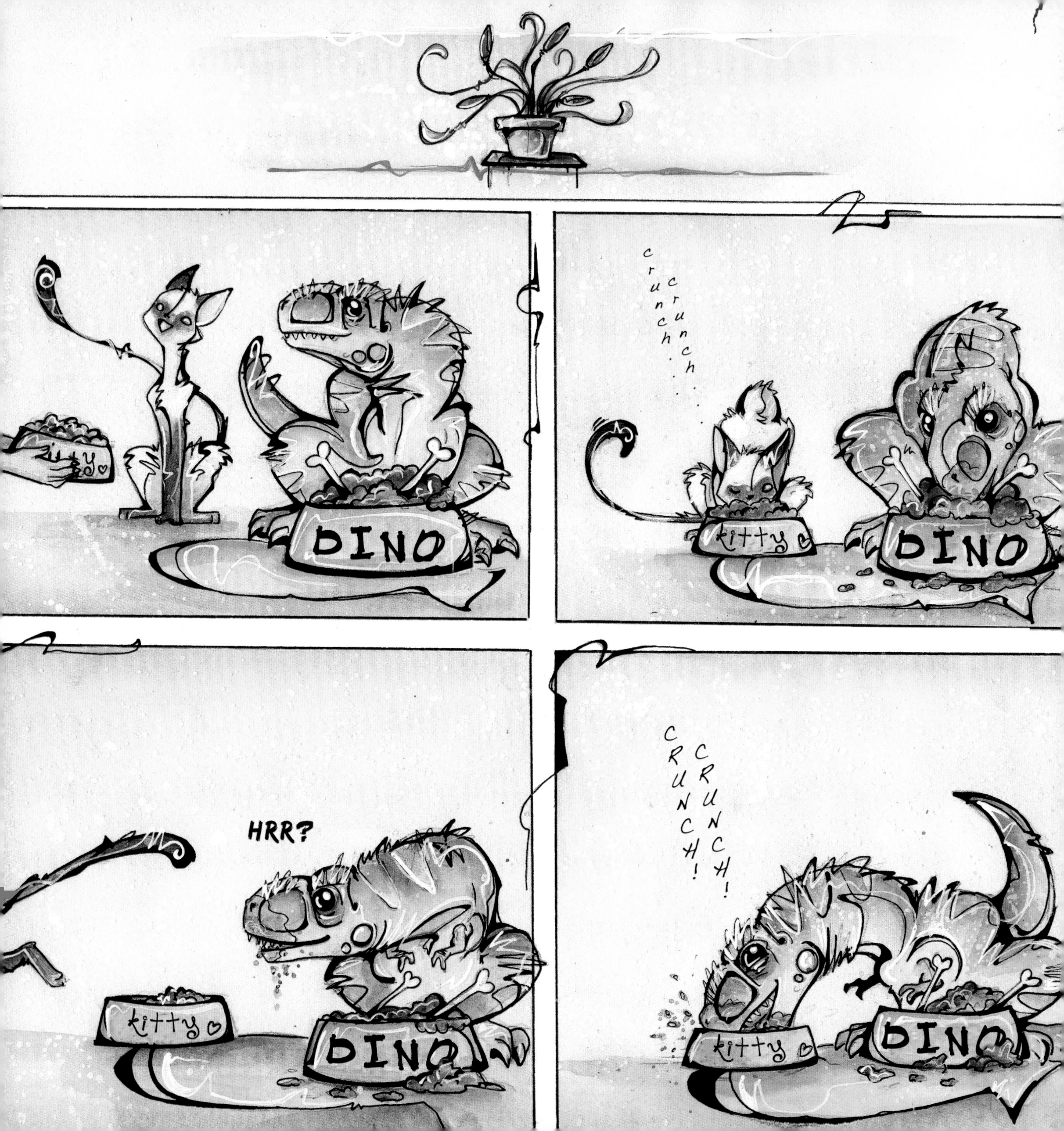
kitty
DINO
crunch crunch...
kitty
DINO
HRR?
kitty
DINO
CRUNCH! CRUNCH!
kitty
DINO

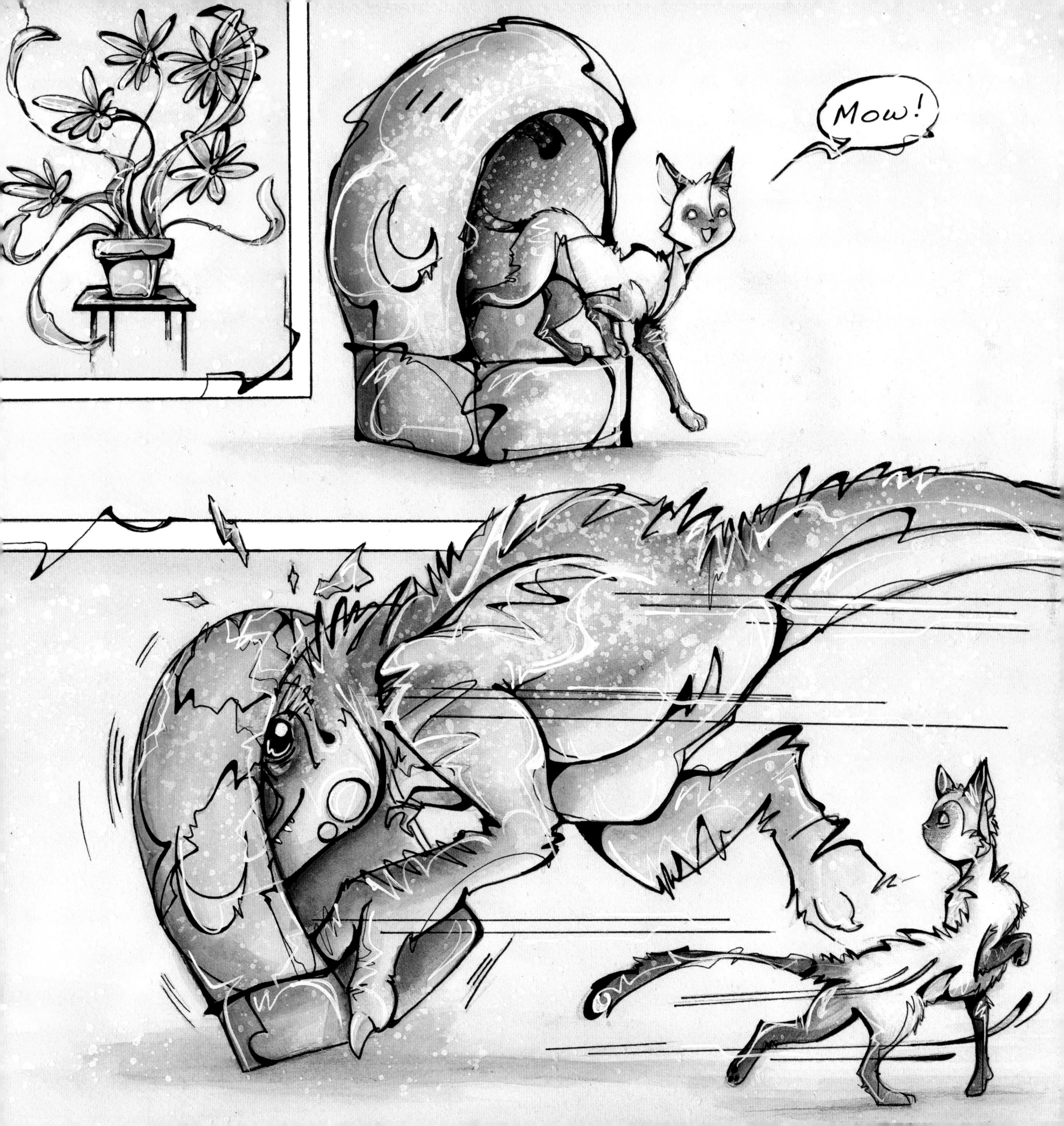
Mow!

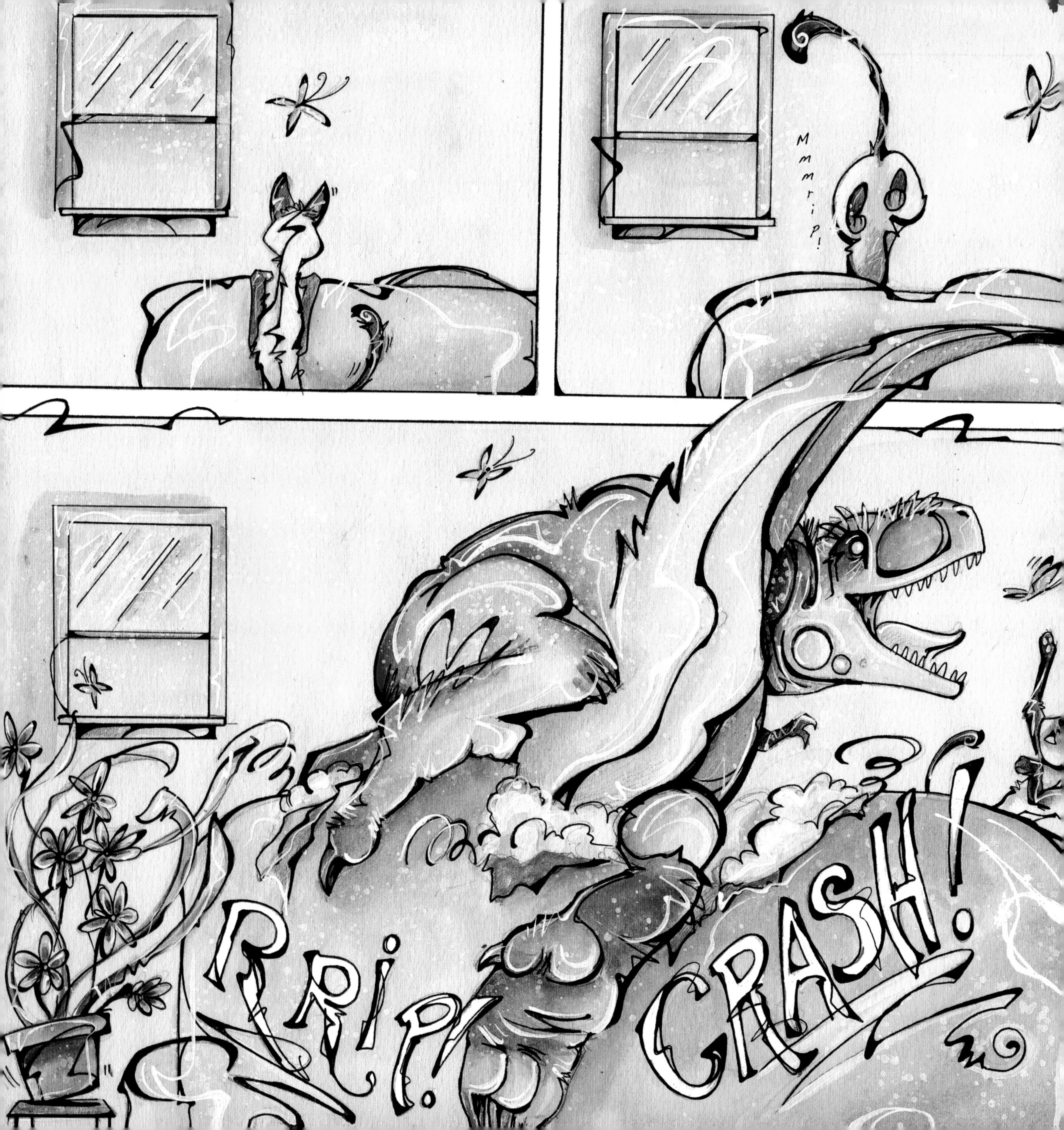
Mmmrip!
RRIP!
CRASH!

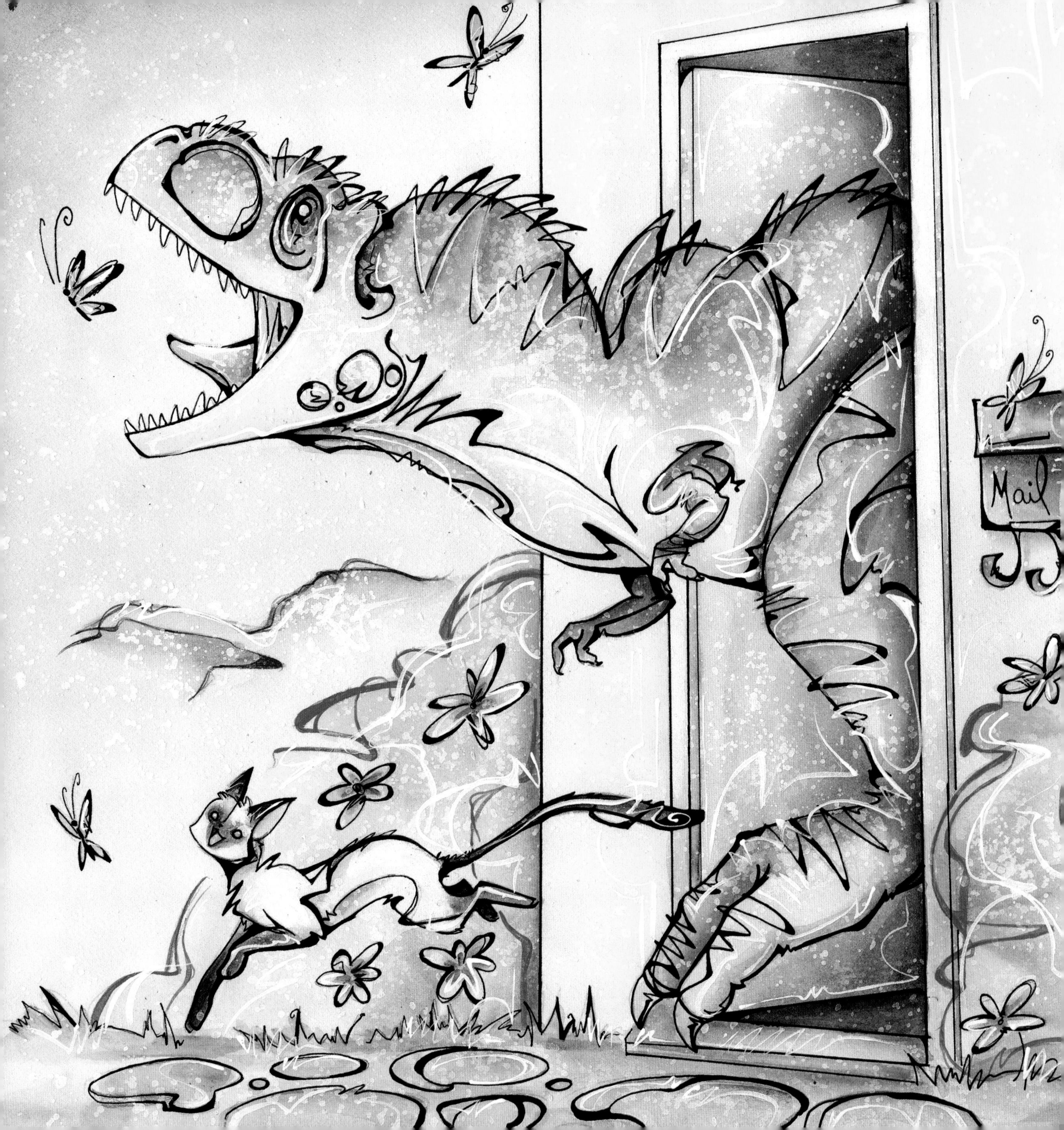
Mail

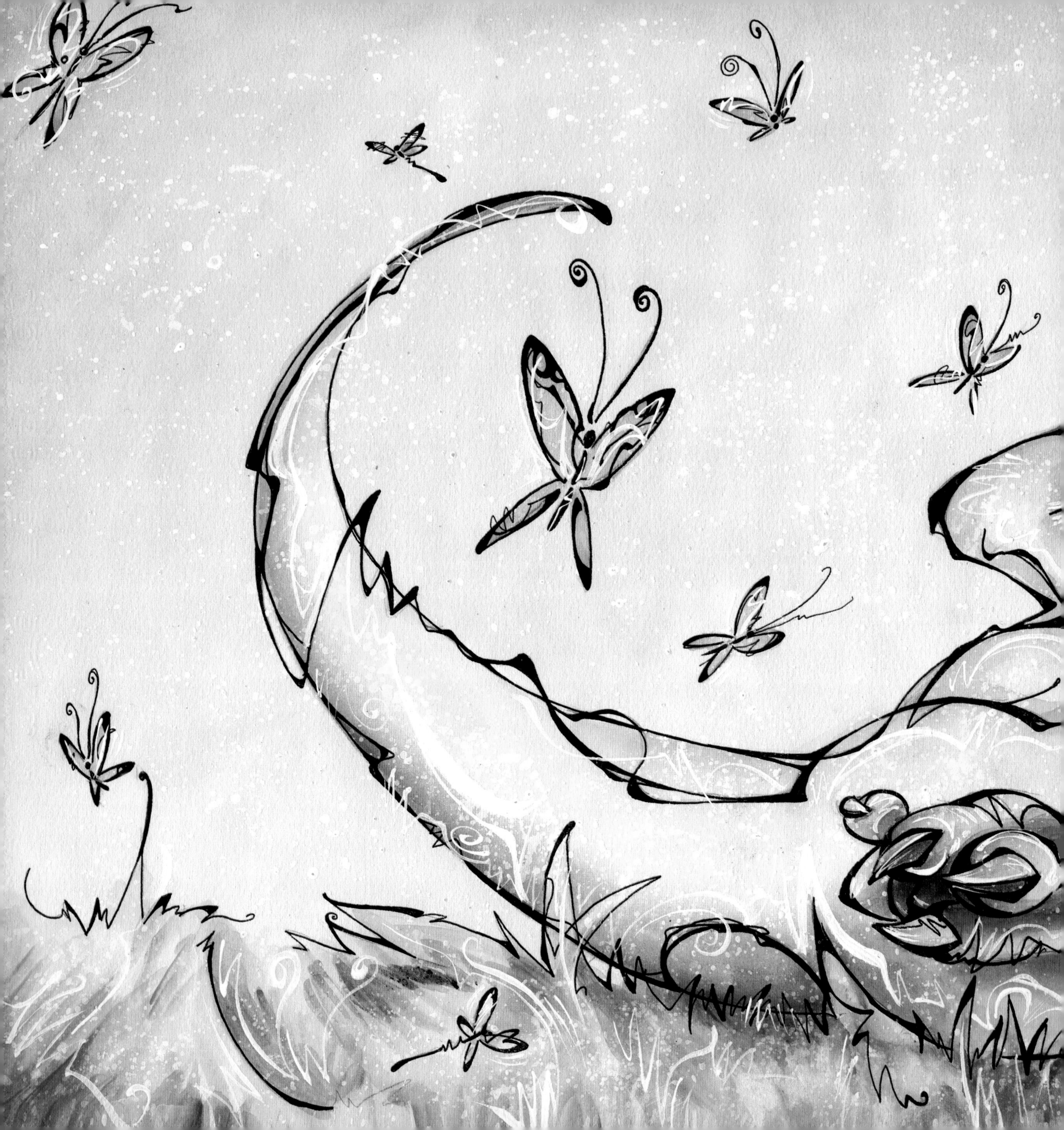

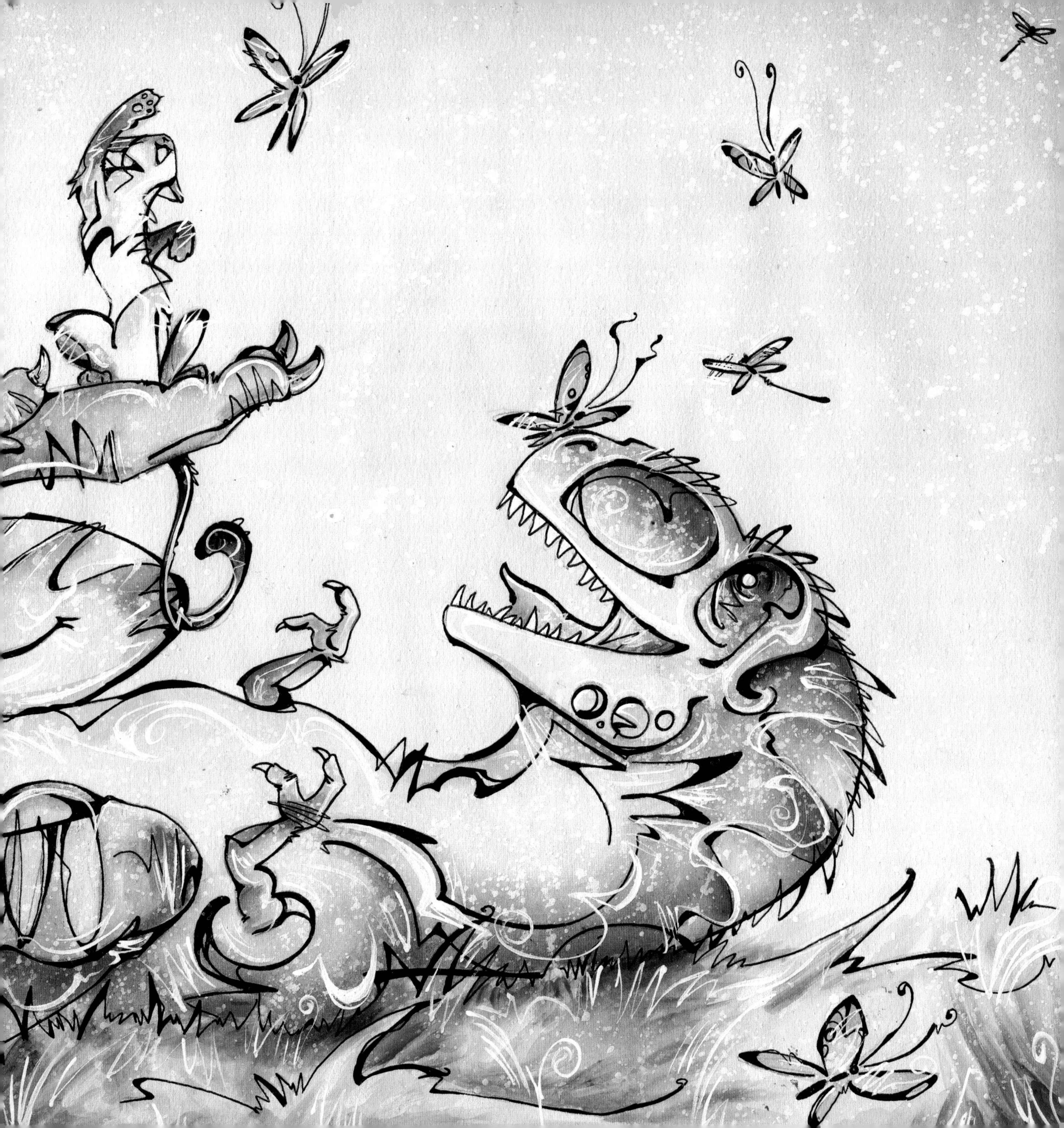

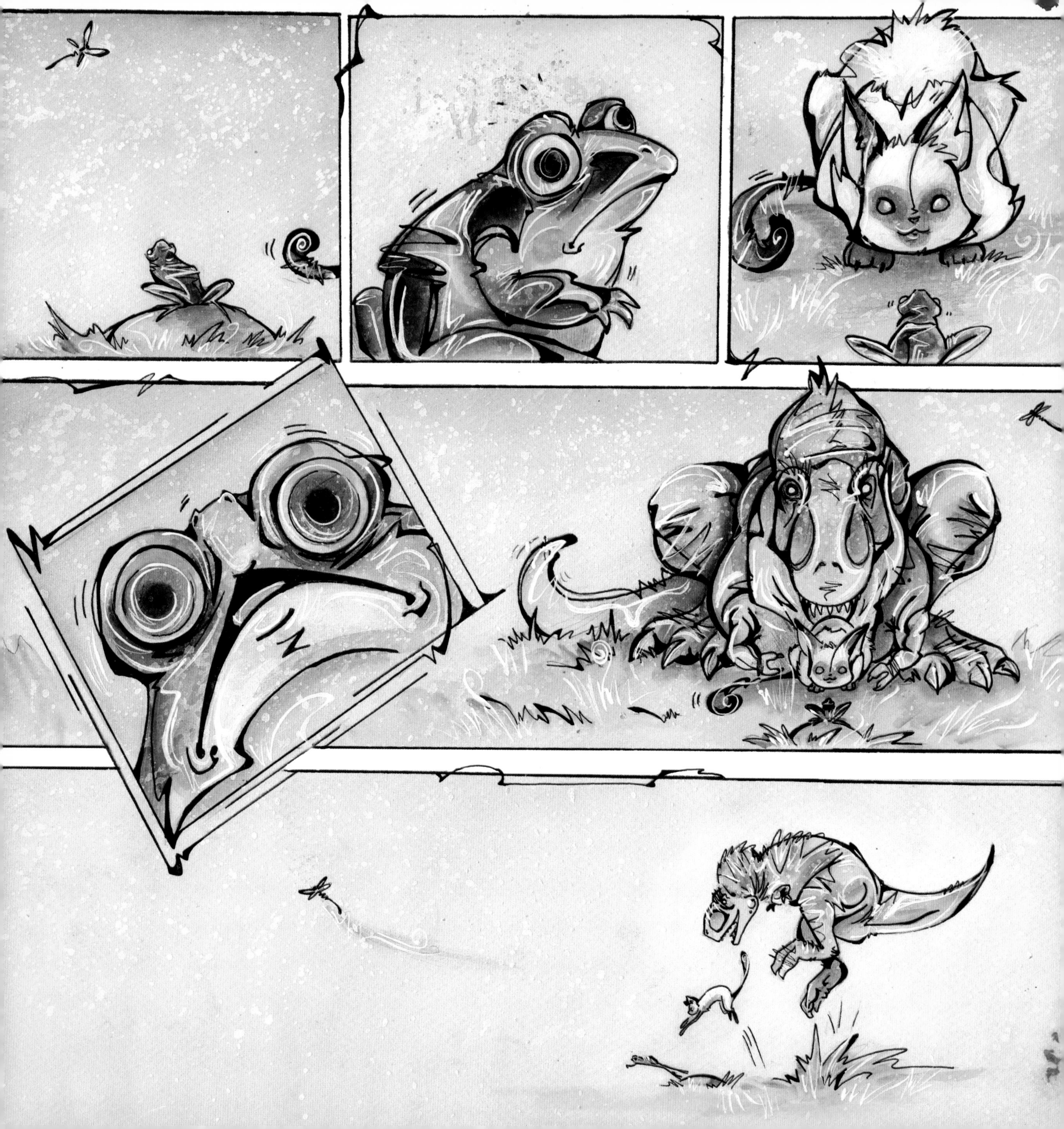

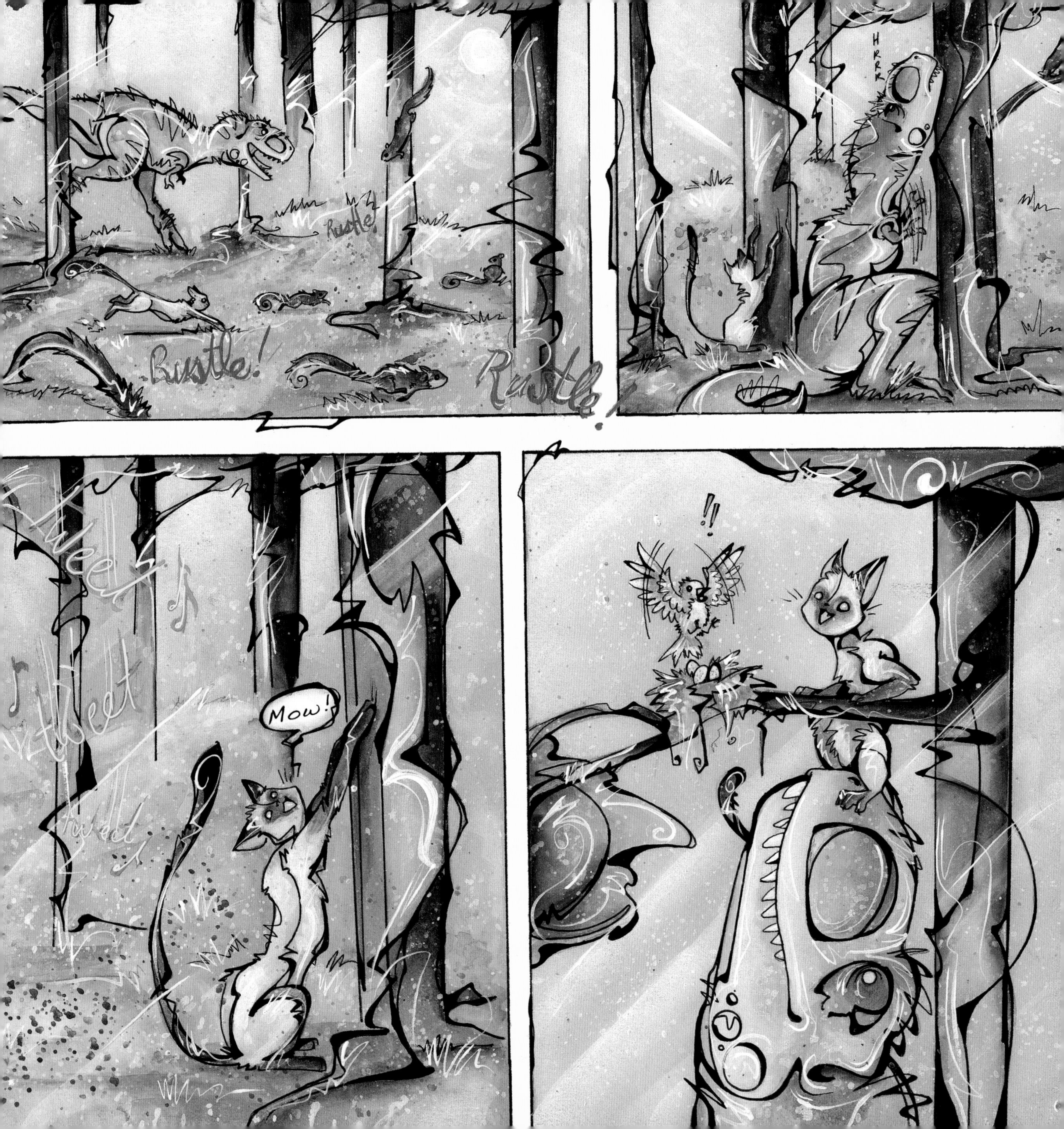
Rustle!
Rustle!
Rustle!
HRRR
Tweet
tweet
tweet
Mow!
!!

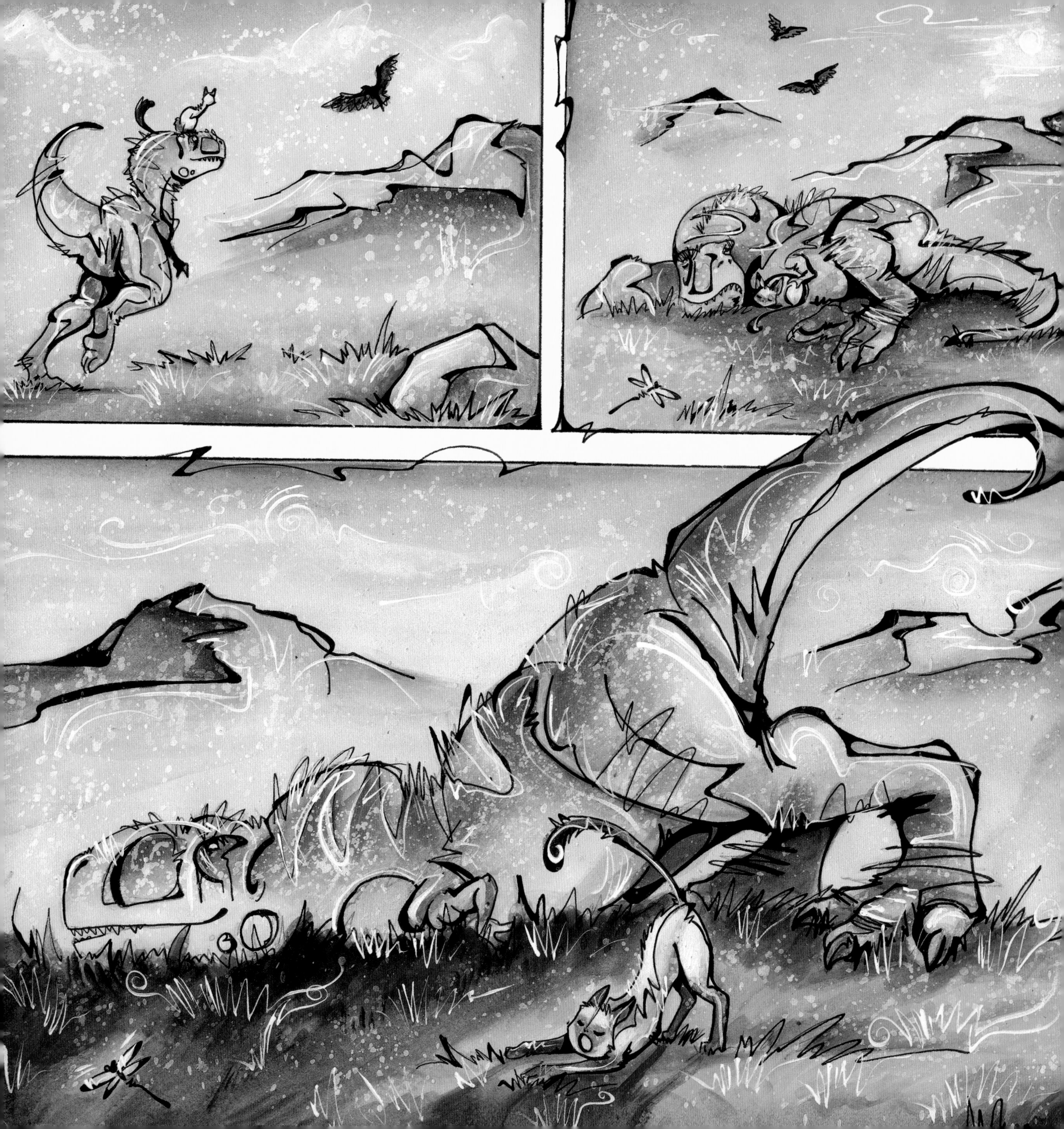

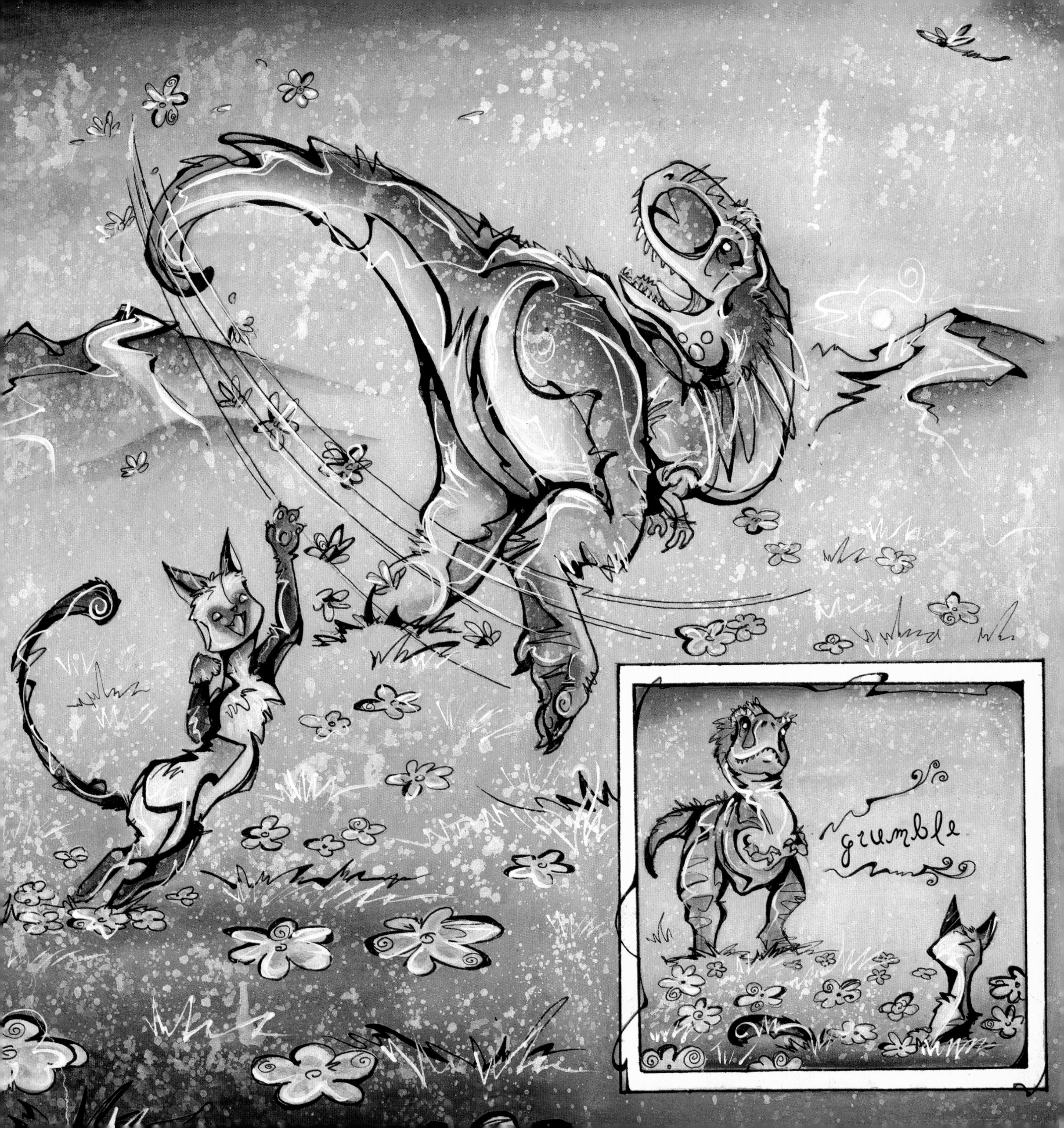
grumble

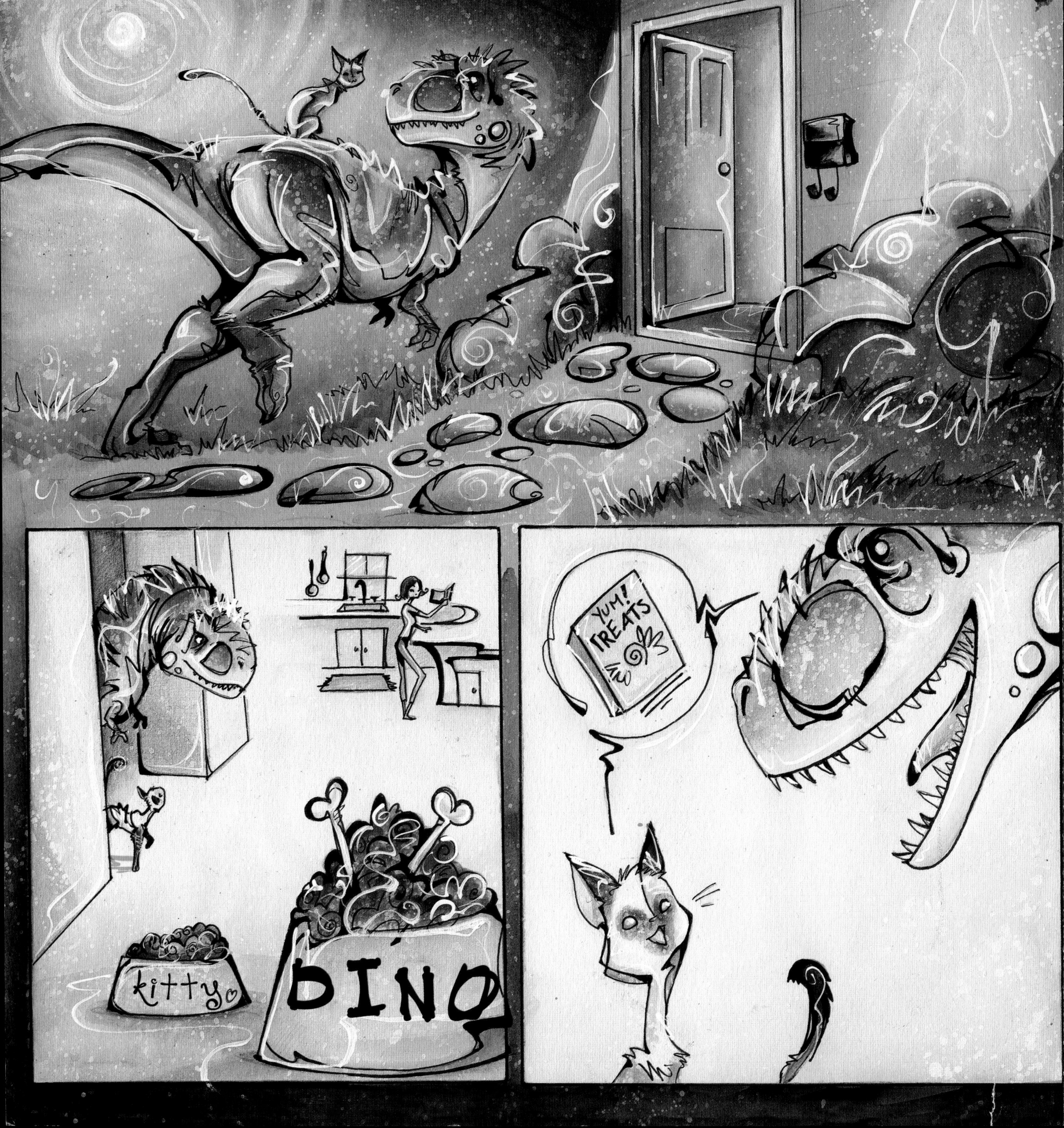
kitty
DINO
YUM! TREATS

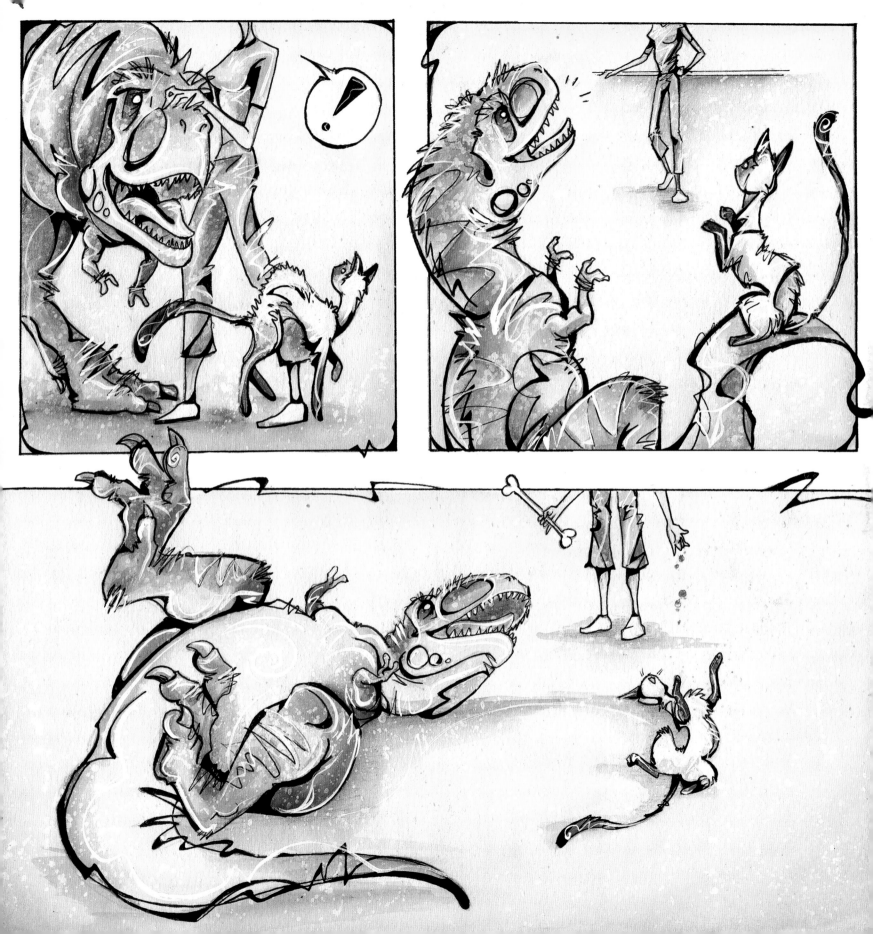

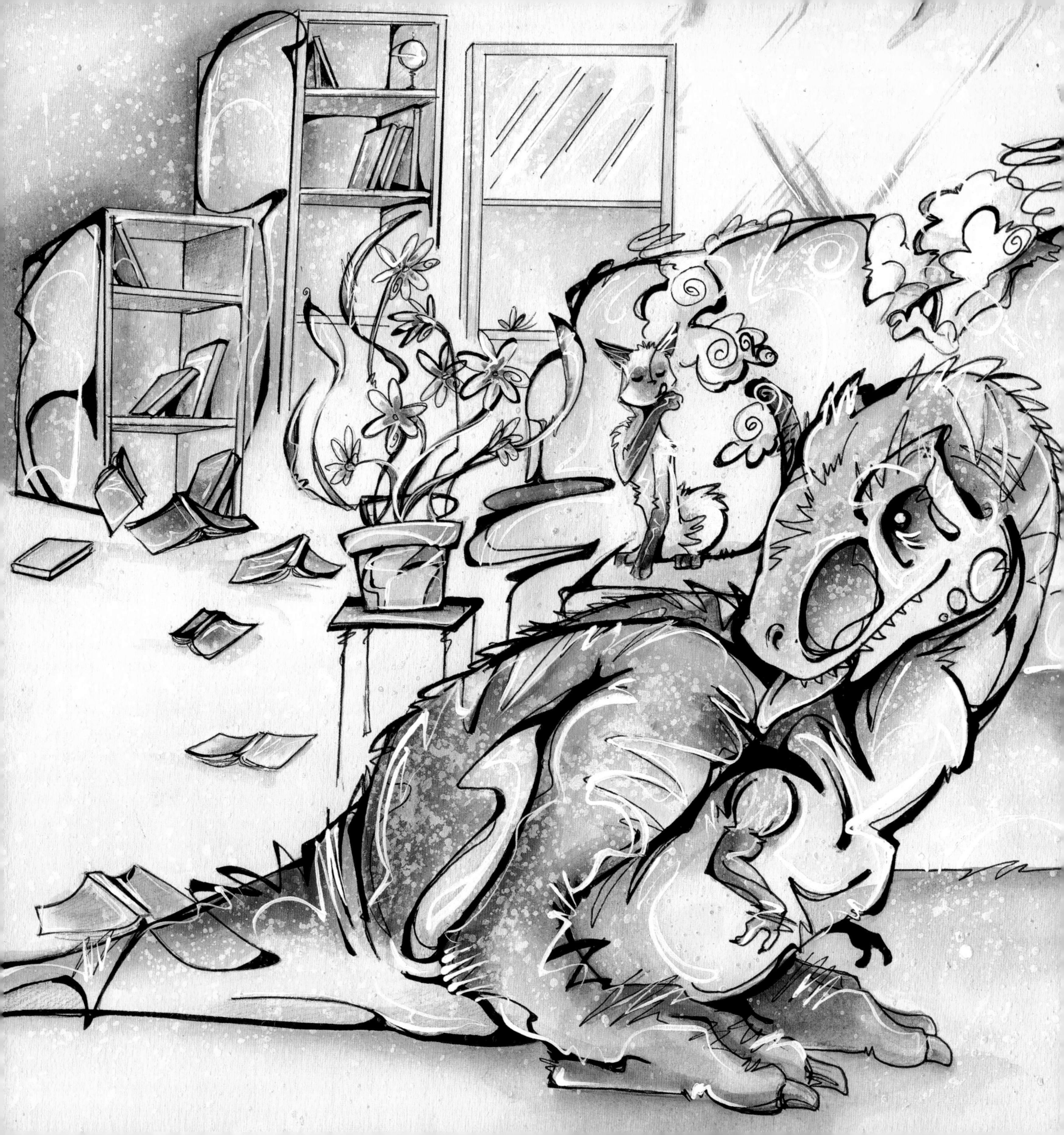

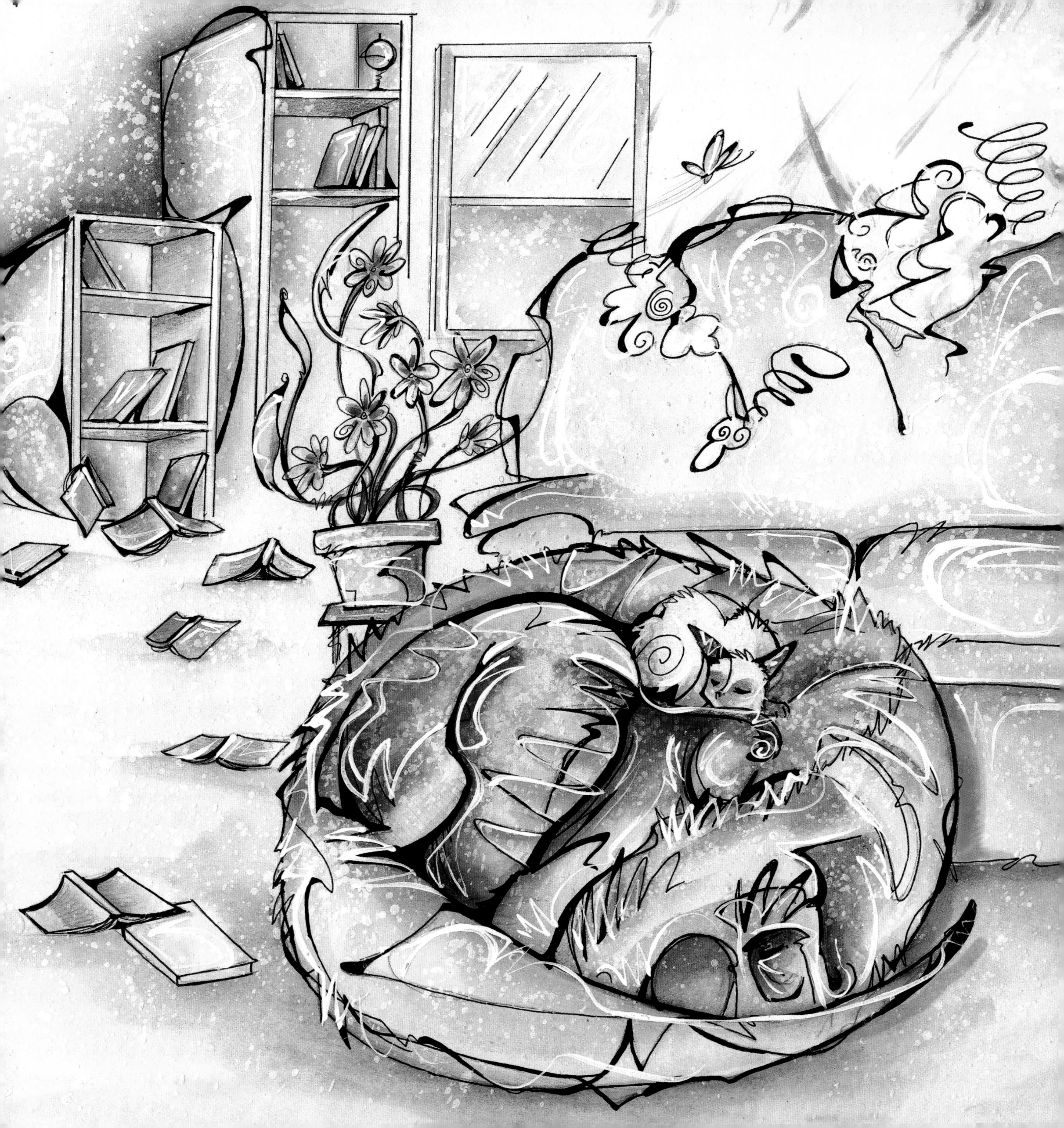

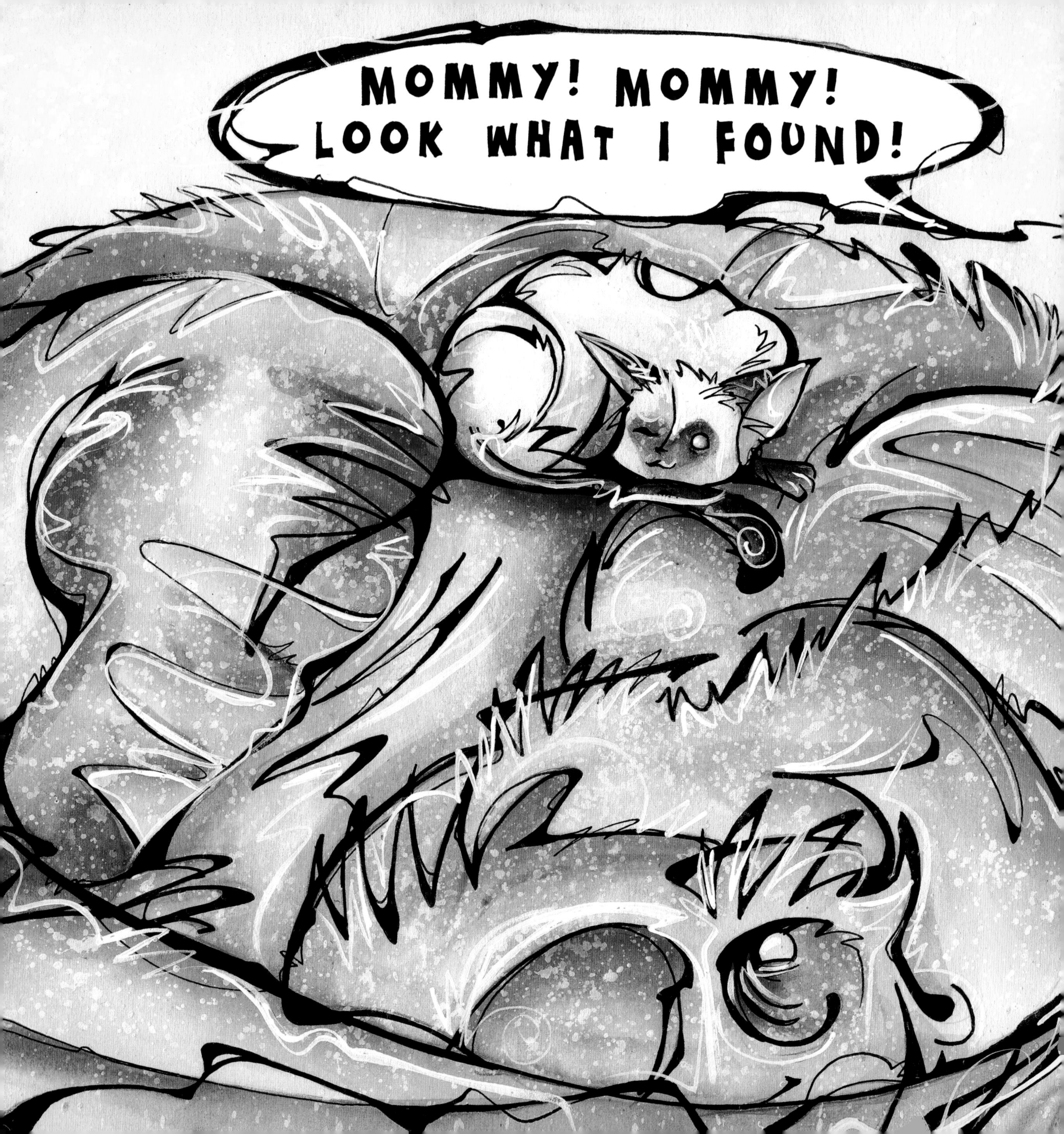
MOMMY! MOMMY! LOOK WHAT I FOUND!

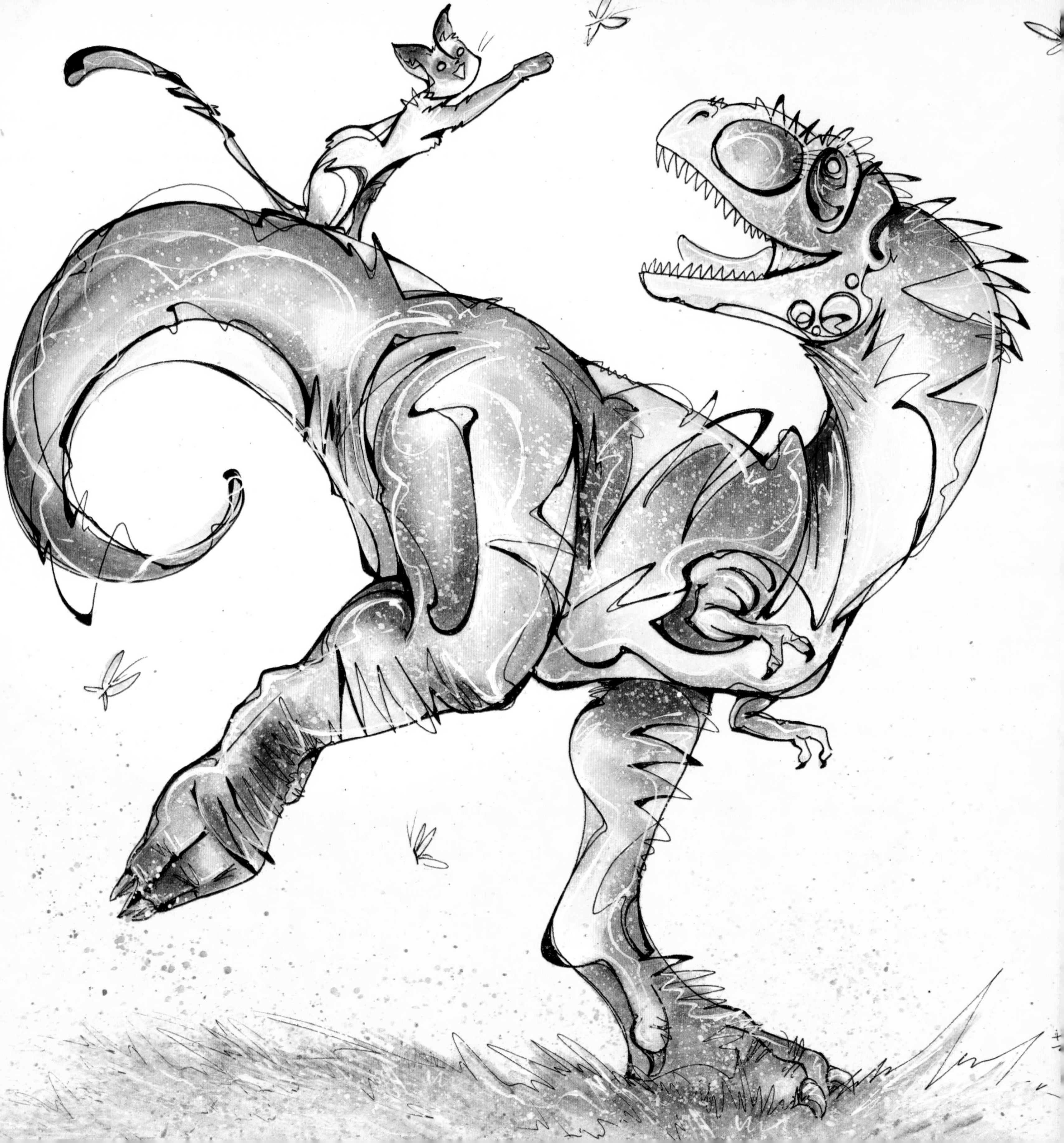

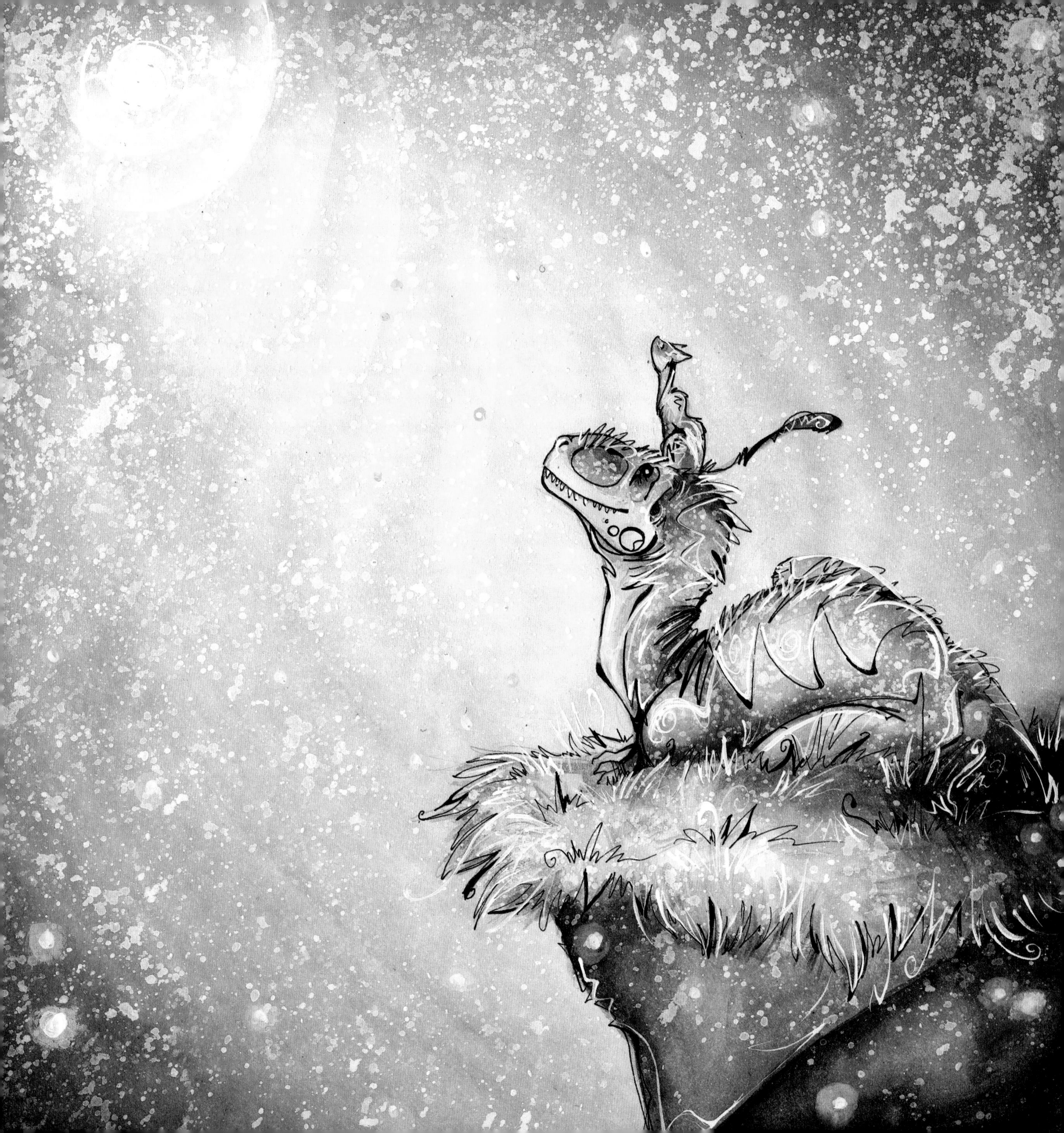

Illustrated by Sara Richard

Yen Press
Hachette Book Group
237 Park Avenue, New York, NY 10017

www.HachetteBookGroup.com
www.YenPress.com

Yen Press is an imprint of Hachette Book Group, Inc.
The Yen Press name and logo are trademarks of Hachette Book Group, Inc.

First Yen Press Edition: April 2012

ISBN: 978-0-316-13351-7

Library of Congress Control Number: 2011940406

10 9 8 7 6 5 4 3 2 1

SC

Printed in China

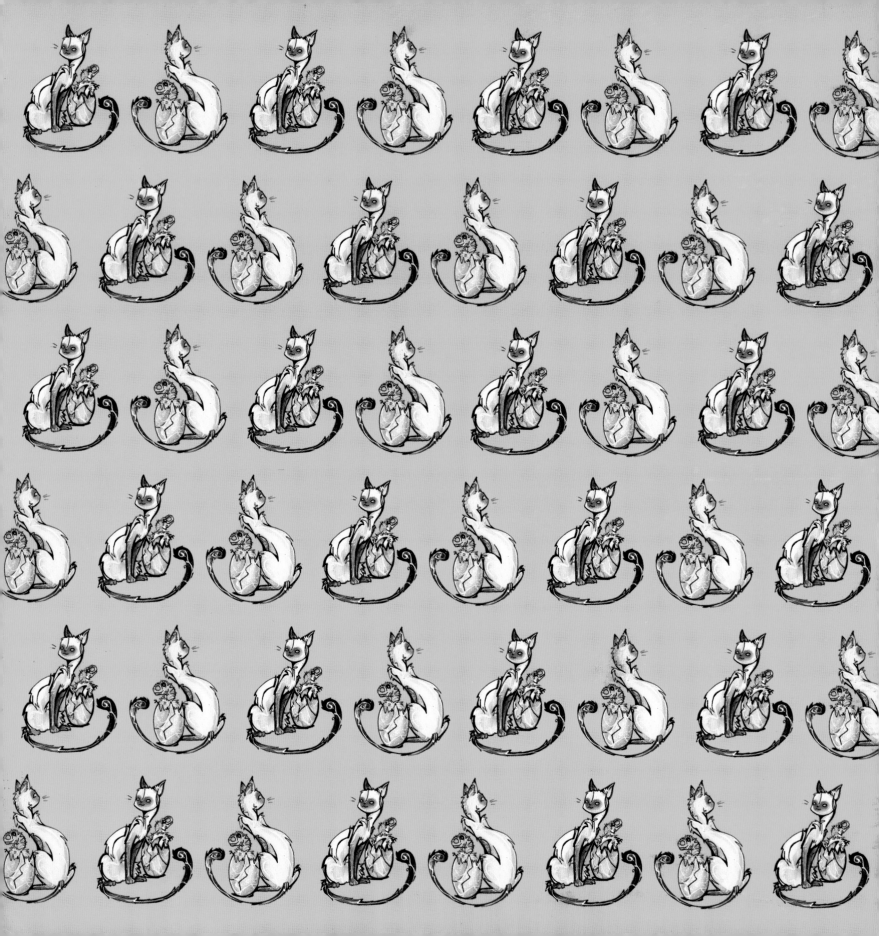